W9-CEL-615
Over the Wall
CHRIS FABRY

TYNDALE HOUSE PUBLISHERS, INC., CAROL STREAM, ILLINOIS

Over the Wall

CHRIS FABRY

Visit Tyndale's exciting Web site at www.tyndale.com

Over the Wall

Designed by Stephen Vosloo

Edited by Lorie Popp

Library of Congress Cataloging-in-Publication Data

Fabry, Chris, date.
Over the wall / Chris Fabry.
p. cm. — (RPM ; #2)
Summary: When Jamie is accepted at an elite NASCAR training school sponsored by a competing racing team, her parents try to get her to trust God to help her decide what to do.
ISBN-13: 978-1-4143-1265-1 (sc : alk. paper)
ISBN-10: 1-4143-1265-2 (sc : alk. paper)
[1. Automobile racing—Fiction. 2. Family life—North Carolina—Fiction. 3. Foster home care—Fiction. 4. NASCAR (Association)—Fiction. 5. Christian life—Fiction. 6. North Carolina—Fiction.] I. Title.
PZ7.F1178Ov 2007
[Fic]—dc22 2007011380

Printed in the United States of America

13 12 11 10 09 08 07
7 6 5 4 3 2 1

This book is dedicated to
Manny and Sheri Saldana, 3/11/07.
Through twists and turns,
may he always make your path clear.

"When the helmet goes on we're all equal. It doesn't matter whether you're a boy or a girl, 13 years old or 30. I'm a race car driver and that's it."

Michelle Theriault

"Stuff happens pretty quick. This time a year ago, I was testing the 16 car for Biffle and that was just a dream come true. . . ."

David Ragan

"Circumstances may appear to wreck our lives and God's plans, but God is not helpless among the ruins. God's love is still working. He comes in and takes the calamity and uses it victoriously, working out his wonderful plan of love."

Eric Liddell

Chapter 1
Ambulance Chase

"MOM, SOMETHING AWFUL has happened," Jamie Maxwell said, her voice shaking. Her hands were also shaking, almost too much to hold her cell phone as she hurried toward Chad Devalon's crashed car.

"Where are you?" her mother said, her voice even and unemotional, though Jamie could tell she was trying hard to stay in control.

Jamie had said nothing to her parents about her test drive in the Devalon car. She now knew that had been a mistake, and she'd hear it from both her mom and her dad when she saw them.

"I'm headed over to the hospital in a few minutes," Jamie said. "Could you meet me at Memorial?"

Her mom hesitated. "Are you all right?"

"I'm fine, Mom."

"Okay, we'll go right over there."

Jamie had beaten the others calling 911 when Chad Devalon crashed, telling the dispatcher their location at the track as the car teetered on its top in the infield. Chad's father, Butch Devalon, and the owner of the Devalon racing team, Shane Hardwick, raced toward the car along with the track manager, who carried a fire extinguisher.

"Chad!" Butch Devalon shouted, and Jamie thought it was the worst sound in the world to hear a father yell his child's name into a wrecked car.

Chad wasn't talking or moving that she could tell—a bad sign.

Mr. Devalon fumbled with the window net, trying to reach the six-point harness.

"Hold up," Mr. Hardwick said, releasing the window net easily.

"He's right," Jamie said. Her voice sounded strange, as if even speaking to someone who'd been in racing as long as these two was sacrilegious. Something inside took over, and she spoke, her voice stronger. "We should get the car off its top before you release him. You unbuckle that strap, and he's going to slam straight into the roof."

The track manager agreed. "Yeah, I'll get my truck." He returned with a Ford F-250, spinning his tires in the infield grass, a chain clanking in the bed.

By then, the swirling siren of the ambulance [illegible] over the track like a song.

"I don't need no ambulance," Chad muttered.

"Just hang in there, Son," Mr. Devalon said.

Jamie had seen the swagger and the strut of Butch Devalon nearly all her life. Her dad had raced against him, first in trucks, then moving their way up the NASCAR ladder to the cup races. When Mr. Devalon didn't finish first or even in the top 10, he was still the picture of self-confidence. Every step said, *I'm number one, even if I didn't win today.* In interviews, he made sure everyone knew the other guy never actually *won* the race—he *lost* it. He'd made a mistake or the team had done something wrong. He let everyone know he should have been in the winner's circle—and would be next time.

However, the swagger was gone—at least temporarily—as Mr. Devalon told his son to keep quiet. He seemed scattered, not knowing what to say or do.

"Blood's running to my head," Chad said, a little stronger now.

The track manager hooked the chain to the car and gently pulled it until the wheels slammed onto the grass.

Butch Devalon unhooked the harness and popped the steering wheel, but the roof was so dented that

Jamie wondered if they could squeeze Chad through the opening.

She turned and waved at the ambulance as it came through the front gate and onto the track. When she looked back, they had Chad sitting on the ground and were taking off his helmet.

The paramedics arrived and moved everyone away. Chad protested louder now, telling the men he was fine and there was no reason for them to be here. They pointed a light at his eyes and tried to keep him still, but he kept pushing them away.

"Let 'em take a look at you," Mr. Hardwick said. "It's for your own good."

"I'm telling you, I'm okay," Chad said. But when he tried to stand, he screamed in pain and his legs gave way.

The paramedics put him on a gurney and loaded him into the ambulance.

Butch Devalon got in the back with Chad and glanced at Jamie. He tried to smile, but lines of worry creased his face.

Jamie ran through the gate and up the hill to her car. Her cell phone rang as she pulled out behind the ambulance.

"Jamie, it's Cassie," her friend said. Her voice felt like a cool breeze on a sweltering day. "I heard something was wrong."

"How did you hear that?" Jamie said.

"Your mom called the prayer tree, and we're at the top of the list. What's going on?"

The prayer tree. Cassie made it sound like a living thing. Basically it was a list of names and phone numbers people at their church called when somebody found out they had a disease or went into rehab or had a teenager in trouble. Jamie called it the "gossip bush" just to make her mom mad. As far as she knew, this was the first time she had made the list, though she figured the guy in Florida, Tim Carhardt, had been on one of the branches.

Cassie Strower was Jamie's best friend. As kids they'd spent summer nights camping out and winter nights at sleepovers. They still had their nails done together on special occasions, but they'd grown apart the more time Jamie spent racing. Cassie was the "perfect" daughter. A strong Christian. She was the kind of girl Jamie figured her mom *wished* she had. That halo over her head was the only thing Jamie didn't like about Cassie. She had a dependence on God that Jamie knew she would *never* have.

"I can't talk now, Cassie. I'm on my way to the hospital. Just pray for Chad. He's been in an accident at the track."

"Got it," Cassie said.

Chapter 2
Discovery

TIM CARHARDT STARED at the small suitcase on his bed. The zipper was stuck halfway, so he couldn't get it open or closed. He'd taped the back of it so it wouldn't flop open. The bottom was frayed from use and smelled like Tyson's closet—which smelled a lot like smoky cotton balls.

Tyson stuck his head in the door. "We're headed over to Wal-Mart. You need anything?"

Since Tyson and his wife had discovered Tim was moving to North Carolina, they'd been nicer. Vera had even taken the stickers off most of the food in the refrigerator. The ones that said *Vera's, do not touch.*

Tim shook his head and Tyson shut the door. Tim could count on one hand the number of times the guy had asked if he needed anything. Most of the time

Tim felt like an unwanted pimple (and what pimple is wanted?) in their lives. He was looking forward to getting away, not just from them but from the trouble he'd found in Tallahassee.

The truck fired up outside. Every time it did, Tim shivered because it was his dad's truck, and the sound reminded him that his dad was gone and never coming back. But his life was about to change big-time, and he couldn't help but think things would get better.

There wasn't much to pack. Mostly just his clothes, and he didn't have many. Two pairs of jeans. A few T-shirts. Underwear. He'd thought about starting to shave, but every time he passed the razors and shaving cream at the drugstore, he'd gotten cold feet. Those commercials on TV made shaving look like it was a breeze, but he'd tried it once with one of Tyson's old razors and cut himself under his nose. He wished he had someone who could show him how to do it, but he wasn't about to ask Tyson. The guy would just laugh and point at what he would call the peach fuzz on Tim's face.

A motor chugged to a stop outside, and Tim's heart jumped. Whenever he heard someone pass, he thought it might be Jeff and his friends who had jumped him. He couldn't wait to get away so he wouldn't have to worry about that. They had taken from him the one thing that meant the most—his dad's diary. When Tim read a few pages, it felt like a connection with his dad. Now all he had was the sweat-stained hat his father had given him with the number and logo of the race crew his dad used to work for.

Something clicked outside. Then a motor revved and gravel spun. Tim looked out and saw a rusted Bronco pulling away from the mailbox. It was the wild-haired mail lady. When they had a lot of bills, she'd secure the mail with a rubber band, and Tim sometimes found her hair wrapped in with it.

He walked to the box and looked up and down the street of the trailer park. Some younger kids played a game of tag next door and squealed. At the end were a few older kids wearing goggles. They used pellet guns and played war, the pellets pinging off the tin trailers and an occasional curse floating down the street. Vera called them the devil kids, and she told Tim to stay away from them. She didn't have to tell him. He liked the thought of shooting a pellet gun but didn't like the thought of getting hit with one.

He grabbed a handful of mail and stepped into the dimly lit kitchen. Pizza coupons. Flyers for half-off LASIK surgery. A big sale at the supermarket—pork chops and Coca-Cola were on the front page. Lots of other junk mail, a few bills, and what looked like a check from the government. Probably the aid his social worker said was supposed to come every month. Tim didn't see any of that money, of course.

However, one envelope caught his eye because it was a dark brown and seemed important. The return address said *McConnel and Brennan, Attorneys at Law* and listed an address in North Carolina. The flap of the envelope was loose in one spot, and Tim pried it open and saw just a portion of the letter. All he could see was . . . *rtin Carhardt estate,* but that's all he needed to send his heart racing.

Tim dropped the rest of the mail on the kitchen table and rushed back to his room. He sat on his bed and stared at the envelope. It was addressed to Tyson Slade, but since it had his dad's name inside, he couldn't help feeling like it was his.

Carefully he tore the rest of the envelope and it ripped. He was going to have a hard time explaining that. He pulled the page out at an angle, but it was difficult because the paper was a lot thicker than regular paper.

The letter said *Dear Mr. Slade* at the top, and Tim shook his head. If these people had any idea what kind of guy Tyson was, they wouldn't have called him *Mr.* Tim had wondered why his dad hadn't prepared a will, but the bigger mystery now was why he'd put Tyson in charge of his money and belongings. Why hadn't his dad put Tim's name on the will?

The first part was a greeting and some legal mumbo jumbo Tim didn't understand. But he read the next paragraph twice.

Per your request, we are writing you instead of the son of the deceased. We hope Timothy is recovering from his devastating loss. This letter is to inform you that we have liquidated the remainder of the Martin Carhardt estate with the exception of the truck you have in your possession, the miscellaneous items in storage, and the other item in the safe-deposit box.

"What item?" Tim said out loud. Tyson had told him his dad didn't even have a will, and here was a letter from a lawyer that showed his dad had left something behind.

The letter continued.

After settling the fees to the various creditors and paying the rest of the loan on the truck, there is a positive balance of $324.56. Unless otherwise instructed, we will mail that sum to you at the end of the six-month waiting period.

The letter ended with instructions on how to get in touch with the lawyers and then added:

We are including a key to the safe-deposit box with this letter. We have a duplicate here at the office if you would prefer having us send you the contents.

Tim looked at the plastic case with the tiny key. He held it up and checked the number, wondering what could be in the box at the bank.

Chapter 3
Hospital

JAMIE FOLLOWED THE AMBULANCE toward the hospital, the radio off for a change. (She usually kept it on a local station and up loud.) She was lost in how great her run around the track had been and how awful she felt about Chad, her thoughts swirling like the lights of the ambulance in front of her. If she hadn't been there, he wouldn't have tried so hard to beat her. The whole thing was her fault.

Another part of her knew that Chad had made his own choices. Everybody made their own way, their own decisions, and Chad had made a bad one. The only question was whether he'd live to make any more.

"I don't know if you can hear me, God," she prayed out loud, "but . . ." Her voice trailed off, and she stopped at a red light, the ambulance rolling right through it.

Who was she kidding? If God was more than just a hope and a dream her parents believed in, she might have kept praying or perhaps promised she'd go to church every Sunday for the rest of her life or become a nun in some convent or never use bad language when she blew a test in biology. Or all of the above.

If God was really up there listening, he'd probably written her off a long time ago for all the stuff she'd done, all the rules she'd broken, all the services she'd missed. She'd promised him those things before—several times—like in New Hampshire when her dad had T-boned the wall doing 185. She and her mom had rushed to the infield care center, hoping, praying. Her mother had been unbelievably calm but still concerned. Her dad had been okay in the end, but Jamie never forgot the promises she'd made to God and how much she'd gone back on every one of them.

"You don't have any reason to help me, because I've done the opposite of everything I promised. But if you'd make Chad okay, I'd appreciate it."

She had a hard time finding a parking space at the hospital, then ran into the emergency waiting room, where Mr. Hardwick paced. Chad's father was at one of the computer terminals giving a lady some information.

"Do you know anything yet?" Jamie said.

"Butch said he was groggy but talking in the ambulance," Mr. Hardwick said. "Chad didn't make a whole lot of sense, but it was clear he didn't want to come here."

Jamie glanced around at the sad faces in the plastic chairs and couldn't blame Chad. The hospital staff concentrated on their jobs, moving from area to area without looking at any of them.

Chad's mom was one of the first people to arrive at the hospital. She went to her husband and hugged him. She was a pretty woman, classy, well dressed, and it looked like she'd just come out of a salon. If Jamie believed what her friends said, Mrs. Devalon had a day spa right in her house and servants that catered to her every need.

Jamie's mom and dad were next through the door. Jamie ran to her mom and hugged her.

"Where's Kellen?" Jamie said when she pulled away, looking past them for her 10-year-old brother.

"We dropped him at a friend's house," her mom said. "Jamie, what happened?"

"I was at the track with the Devalons. Chad had a problem and . . ."

Mr. Hardwick walked up and shook her dad's hand. Jamie knew he could tell something was wrong because he squinted at her. "They didn't know anything about your test run?"

"About what?" Jamie's dad said.

"I rode in one of the Devalon cars at the track," Jamie said. "Just a test to see what my time would be."

Her dad looked like somebody had sucker punched him. "And whose idea was that?"

"It was mine," Butch Devalon said behind him, and Jamie's dad turned. "I wanted to see how she'd do against Chad before I nominated her."

"For what?" her dad said. Then a look of realization came over him. "You want to sponsor . . . ?"

Her mom put a hand on his arm. "Dale, this is not the time or place. We can talk about it later."

"You're right." Her dad nodded and pursed his lips. "Butch, how's Chad doing?"

"He's a tough kid. That six-point harness probably saved his life. But he's banged up. That's for sure."

"What happened?" her mom said.

"Looked like his tire just shredded on turn three. He fought it into the wall, but it got loose and went sideways on him."

"He went airborne?" her dad said.

Mr. Devalon nodded. "He said he closed his eyes as he flipped. Then all he saw were the sparks from the racetrack and the grass and dirt coming at him under the windshield."

"Well, I'm thankful he's okay," Jamie's dad said, then looked at Jamie, as if he were saying, *That could have been you.*

Nurses and staff ran down the hall, and Mrs. Devalon looked at her husband across the room. "Something's wrong with Chad."

Chapter 4
Bad News

SOMEONE KNOCKED ON THE DOOR of the trailer, and Tim stuffed the brown envelope under his pillow and quietly walked to the kitchen. A thin curtain blocked the window on the door, but Tim noticed someone standing there, and he froze. It looked like a man, not Vera's friend from down the street who came over and talked and cried with her about her marriage and all her troubles in what Tim called a boo-hoo-woe-is-me session.

The man knocked again and shifted from foot to foot. He took something from his front pocket, dipped his head, and just stood there a few moments. Then he bent over out of Tim's sight, and something plopped against the front door before he walked down the creaky steps.

Tim inched forward, looking out the

front window at a red SUV parked in front. He finally recognized the lanky frame of the pastor at the local megachurch. The guy who had hired Tim and then fired him after Tim had gotten into a fight with a guy named Jeff and his goony friends.

When the man pulled out, Tim opened the door and something fell into the room. He wasn't sure, but it looked a lot like his dad's diary with a page paper-clipped to the front.

Tim,

I'm sorry I missed you. I heard about your run-in again with Jeff and his friends, and I have a friend at the reptile park who found this floating in one of the ponds. I figured you'd want it back.

I've been thinking a lot about your future. If you ever need to talk or just a safe place to go, please call me.

Tim saw the pastor's name and number, crumpled the note, and threw it in the trash. He couldn't believe one of the gators hadn't chomped the notebook. It was three times its normal size—water will do that to paper, get inside it and expand it. He'd heard that in his science class one day when he was halfway paying attention. (Tim remembered a joke of his dad's, that he was too poor to pay attention.) He flipped through the pages and saw the faded writing stained with mud. He couldn't read most of it, but at least he could see some of his dad's writing.

He opened the trash can lid and brushed away some grit and grime from the pages, then closed the cover and ran a hand over his dad's name on the front.

I guess not everybody in churches are jerks, Tim thought.

The phone rang and Tim picked up the cordless handset. Tyson didn't have caller ID. He said they were lucky to afford phone service, let alone all the bells and whistles. It was Lisa, the social worker he'd been talking to since he'd moved to Florida.

"I have some bad news, Tim. The Maxwells have had an emergency and need to reschedule the trip."

"You mean they're not coming?" Tim said. "They don't want me, do they?"

"No, that's not true," Lisa said quickly. "They're really excited about you coming to live with them, but there was a wreck of some sort, and instead of Dale driving down to pick you up tomorrow, he's going to have to push that back."

"What kind of wreck?"

"I'm not sure, but you have to believe me that this

doesn't have anything to do with their wanting you up in North Carolina."

"When will I go?"

"I don't know yet, but I should hear from them tomorrow."

Tim got quiet, chewing on the inside of his cheek. He chewed the thin line of skin when he was nervous or scared or felt bad about something. He even did it in his sleep and sometimes woke up biting down.

"Tim, are you okay?" Lisa said. "Is something wrong?"

He walked into his room and sat on the bed, pulling the lawyer's letter out and turning it in his hand. "No, I'm all right. Tell them they can take their time. And if they have second thoughts, I'll understand."

"They're not having second thoughts. Just get your stuff packed and be ready to go."

I already got my stuff packed, Tim thought. *Took me two minutes.* "I'll be ready," he said.

Chapter 5
A Dangerous Sport

JAMIE SAT IN A PLASTIC CHAIR, a leg pulled to her chest, and watched people pace in the waiting room. Her dad had gone down the hall to make a call, and when he returned, he didn't make eye contact, which was a sure sign that he was ticked. She wondered what he'd say when they got home, but at the moment it was just a waiting game to find out about Chad. The doctors hadn't come out, and they shooed his mother out of the room soon after all the commotion.

Jamie's mom sat with an arm around her, not saying much. She'd given her a look and a "You okay?" That was about it, and it was fine with Jamie. She really didn't want to talk to anyone.

The sounds of cell phone rings (tweets and buzzes and "We Will Rock You") broke the uncomfortable silence.

That and a TV mounted on the wall showing a game show. People stared at it, drawn like human moths to the glow of the screen.

Why do they even have a TV here? Jamie thought.

One man had his hand wrapped, and blood oozed through the gauze. He pointed at the screen and talked to it, giving the contestant advice. A man in the corner leaned forward with his elbows on his knees while his two children fought over toys in a play area. His boy held a bloody bandage over a wound on his head while he tried to put a couple of LEGO blocks together, and his daughter had discovered a dirty-faced doll.

Butch Devalon wandered toward the front window and stared through long vertical blinds at the orange glow above the mountains.

Jamie went to get a drink from the water fountain, and when she passed by him, she paused. "You haven't heard any more, have you?" She knew he hadn't because she'd been watching him the whole time, but it was the only thing she could think of to say.

"I don't know what all the fuss was about," he growled. "I guess they're giving him the once-over, or maybe it's a twice-over now. When those doctors get ahold of you, they're like snapping turtles."

"How so?" Jamie said.

"You ever see one of those at Lake Norman?

A turtle will bite and hang on for dear life. Won't let go for anything."

Jamie didn't like the comparison of doctors to turtles, especially since they were trying to help Chad, but she wasn't about to say anything.

Mr. Devalon got a far-off look and spoke as if it didn't matter whether anyone was around or not. "You kids think you're invincible, that nothing can touch you. All it takes is one mistake. . . ."

"Chad didn't do anything wrong," Jamie said. "You said yourself it was the tire—"

"Mistake, accident, whatever you want to call it. It only takes one."

"Then why do you let Chad race?" she said.

"Because it's what he wants to do, just like you. It's all he talks about or thinks about. If he's not down at the garage, he's at the track or working on some car. Or racing one of those video games."

"Maybe we're going too fast—trying to move up and all," Jamie said.

The man frowned, and lines formed around his mustache and all over his face like an expressway around some big city. "Just remember this, standing here in a hospital waiting room. This is a dangerous sport, young lady." He shook his head and stared out the window. "I shouldn't have brought you in on this."

"Why did you?"

"Thought it would light a fire under Chad."

"As if he needs that," Jamie said.

"He leaves a lot on the track. Gets tentative. Brakes when he ought to speed up. I wanted to push him, and I've never seen him race harder than when you're on the track."

"He doesn't want to lose to a girl."

"I guess. I can't blame him. But look where it got him." He sighed and rubbed his eyes with a thumb and index finger.

"So you were using me to get him to speed up?" Jamie said. "Looks like it worked. But that means you never intended to give me a shot in the first place."

Butch Devalon shrugged, and a look of despair crept over him. Jamie had never seen that in all the years she'd watched him race. He always looked so confident and sure. It was almost enough to make her feel sorry for him.

"Maybe if Chad doesn't make it back, I'll have you—"

"Don't talk that way," Jamie interrupted. "I'm surprised he didn't want the ambulance to take a spin around the track before they brought him here. He'll probably want to do the same on the way home."

Mr. Devalon smiled, but his heart wasn't in it. "I hope so."

Jamie turned and leaned against the glass, her arms folded. "Earlier you said you were going to nominate me for something. For what? What were you talking about?"

Before he could answer, a swinging door opened, and a man in a white coat walked out. "I'm looking for the Devalons."

Mr. and Mrs. Devalon walked over and shook the man's hand. It was clear the doctor didn't watch NASCAR because he didn't light up like most people did when they saw a driver. The doctor spoke in a hushed voice, but the waiting room was so quiet (other than the TV) that Jamie could hear. "Chad's awake and talking now. If you want to see him, you can go on back."

"What was the problem earlier?" Mrs. Devalon said.

"He passed out when he tried to get up too quickly. It may be that he was just light-headed."

"Can he go home?" Mr. Devalon said.

"We want to run some more tests and keep him overnight. Only as a precaution. There may have been some internal injuries, and we want to make sure he's 100 percent."

Chad would not like staying in any hospital room, even if they had cable and he could watch SPEED.

No sooner had the Devalons left than the waiting

room door opened and Cassie and her mother hurried inside. Cassie rushed to Jamie and hugged her. They went to the corner, where they were semialone, and Jamie told her friend everything that had happened.

"You never told your parents about this, did you?" Cassie said.

Jamie rolled her eyes. "And I'm gonna be in big trouble. I should give up my racing dreams and settle for a life of pizza delivery."

"It's not that bad," Cassie said. "Your parents will forgive you . . . after they lock you up for a year. Besides, you like pizza."

Jamie smiled. Cassie was super spiritual, but she also had a good sense of humor. She wiped her eyes and looked at her friend. "What happens if Chad isn't okay? He could have been killed out there today."

Cassie nodded. "I've been scared for you ever since I saw you in those little cars at the summer shoot-out thing—"

"Bandoleros."

"Yeah. I just don't see how anybody can race and not think about God."

There it was. The God factor Jamie had been waiting for. In almost every conversation with Cassie and every time they went to the mall or out for something to eat at the Pit Stop, God came up. Not in a pushy way like someone trying to sell you soap or jewelry from a catalog but as a natural part of the conversation.

"Cassie, do you ever *not* think about God?" Jamie said with a hint of a smile.

Cassie remained serious. "I just think about guys like Chad and how far they are from God. I mean, I don't care how many cars you have, how big your house is, or how famous your dad is—if your life ends, what good is all that?"

Jamie knew they were talking about Chad, but she couldn't help thinking about herself. She was going after all those things with her life.

Butch Devalon returned to the waiting room as the youth pastor from church, Pastor Gordon, came in. Pastor Gordon walked up to him and shook hands.

"How did he know about this?" Jamie whispered to Cassie.

"I called him," she said.

"Our entire church has been praying for you and your family," Pastor Gordon said to Butch Devalon. "I'd be glad to pray with you right now if you'd like."

Mr. Devalon's gaze darted around the waiting room, and he let go of Pastor Gordon's hand. "We don't need that. Chad's going to be okay."

"I understand," Pastor Gordon said. "I just wanted you to know we're here and we care."

"Yeah," Butch Devalon said. And he walked away.

Chapter 6
The Nomination

JAMIE OFFERED TO PICK UP Kellen on her way home from the hospital, hoping she could get on her parents' good side. They wanted to stay a little longer at the emergency room and talk with Pastor Gordon, so they took her up on the offer. Pastor Gordon was his usual cheery self. The snub from Butch Devalon didn't seem to bother him.

Kellen was curious, wanting to hear every detail of the crash, but Jamie wasn't in a talkative mood. She knew she treated him like a nuisance most of the time, but what were little brothers for?

"What did you do at Derek's house?" she said, trying to change the subject.

"That's not Derek's house. Derek lives down the street. I was at Paul's."

"Then what did you do with Paul? Play basketball?"

Kellen rolled his eyes. "Don't try to act interested, Jamie. I know you're not."

"I am interested. I ask you about school all the time."

"Why did *you* pick me up?" Kellen said. "You in trouble with Mom and Dad?"

Jamie stared at the road. *How does he figure this stuff out?*

"I'll bet Devalon offered you a spot on his junior race team or something, and they're mad you didn't tell them about it. Right?"

"I'm not on any Devalon team. But thanks for not telling them about what he said down in Daytona."

Kellen looked out the window. "If it gets you killed, Mom and Dad won't thank me."

"I'm not going to get killed."

The message light flickered on the answering machine as they walked inside, and Jamie hit the button. Five people from church had called to find out about the accident, but the last message was an older man interested in Jamie's Legend car. She wrote his number down and hurried to her room when she saw her parents pulling into the driveway.

"Why are you selling the car?" the man asked when she called.

"I'm moving up to a bigger car. I need the money to buy one."

He said he would come by tomorrow to look at it, so she gave him her address. Then she heard footsteps on the stairs and a light knock on her bedroom door. It was her father.

Jamie had always idolized her dad. She shared his love of racing and the adventure of climbing into a car and going as fast as you possibly could. However, she did not like the look on his face.

"We need to talk," her dad said.

"I'm sorry I went behind your back and raced Chad's car," Jamie said quickly, running her words together. "I won't do it again."

Her dad sat on her bed and ran a hand through his thick hair. Funny that her mom wasn't here. Usually when they came down hard on her, they put up a unified front like some military maneuver. Operation Jamie.

"Any change in Chad?" Jamie said before her dad could speak.

"Looks like he's going to be okay."

"That's good, because it was scary seeing that crash, Dad." When she got nervous or was about to be nailed for something, she talked faster. "I've never seen anybody alone on the track get into that kind of accident. Really messed the car up. I don't think they can save it. Of course, with Mr. Devalon's money it doesn't matter. . . ."

Her dad just stared at her until her words slowed and sputtered to a stop like an engine running out of gas.

Then she revved again. "I thought you were going to leave for Florida tonight."

"Got a little sidetracked by what happened. Had to cancel."

"You're not picking that guy up? What's his name?"

"It's Tim Carhardt, and we thought what happened tonight was pretty important. I wanted to drive down and spend some time talking to him on the way back. Guess we'll need to make other arrangements."

Jamie nodded. "Well, Texas is coming up this weekend. Maybe you could—"

Her dad gave her the look that said *Stop talking,* so she did.

"The thing that bothers me isn't that you would drive a Devalon car," her dad said. "And I'm not upset that you would think about joining his team."

"Did Kellen mention it? That little rat. I even thanked him for not telling you about it."

"It doesn't matter where I heard it. The point is,

what really upsets me is that you would keep all this from us."

"I was scared you wouldn't let me, that you'd be mad. And I was right—you *are* mad."

"I'm upset that you thought you had to keep this a secret. I've told you I want to help you be the very best driver you can be."

"You keep secrets from us," Jamie said and regretted it as soon as she said it.

"Like what?"

"Nothing."

"Like what?" her dad said a little firmer this time.

"Like the guy in Florida. You knew way back in December that you wanted him to come live here."

"That's not fair. We didn't even know if it was possible or if he'd agree to come here."

Jamie turned her head, her face hot, pretending that she'd been hurt. Silence filled the room, and she focused on a stack of *NASCAR Illustrated*.

Her dad took a deep breath. "Devalon has suggested you for something."

"He told me he was thinking of signing me to his team. That they might offer me a contract."

"It's not that. You've heard of the Skylar Jennings school, right?"

"They do those ride alongs with NASCAR wannabes. Old guys who can hardly get behind the wheel."

He smiled for a second, which almost felt like a checkered flag waving. One small victory. "Yeah, they do that at tracks around the country. A pretty successful business. But Skylar also teaches rookies and kids whose parents have enough cash. It's expensive, but they say it's worth it."

"What's this got to do with me? I don't even have enough money for a new car."

"A few months ago some owners got together to identify the top prospects around the country, with an eye on diversity, bringing minorities and more female drivers into the program."

Jamie's heart raced, and she sat straight. "Sounds like a good idea."

"The program will last four weeks. It starts in May. Intense classroom instruction. Lots of seat time. They have a few simulators, you'd learn from some of the best PR people, and there are races—"

"Dad, why are you telling me this?"

"Devalon picked you."

She scooted forward, her eyes wide open. "Me?"

"There are already 42 from around the country who've been picked. Most of them are older than you and have more experience. They need one more."

She tried to catch her breath. She had a million questions.

"Devalon and Shane made the decision when

they saw you run Chad's car. They have the last spot. You know how NASCAR is all about leveling the playing field and making things more equal. This is one way they can instruct privately and let the cream rise to the top."

"It sounds like a dream come true," Jamie said.

"There's more." Her dad crossed his legs. "They're keeping score throughout the process. Classroom. On the track. Simulator. The top three drivers at the end of the four weeks get an actual license by NASCAR."

Jamie's mouth dropped open. All she could say was, "Awesome!"

"Obviously those three would have to keep their qualifications up, and they'd still need to work their way through—"

Jamie jumped toward him and threw her arms around him. "Thank you! I can't believe it!"

"Wait a minute. That's the good news. The bad news is that there's school to contend with—"

"I can do some kind of independent study. I'll do homework every night and finish."

"Well, hang on. The cost of the school is covered, but living expenses aren't. Students pay for the hotel and food."

"How much?" Jamie said.

He told her.

"That shouldn't be a problem if I can sell the car."

Her dad ran a hand through his hair. "I guess that's your choice. It's your car. But there's one other problem. A big one."

"What?"

"Your mother."

Jamie's heart fell. "She has to know this is a great opportunity. Once in a lifetime."

"Yeah, she's a smart woman. She knows this is about the best thing that could ever happen to a young driver who wants to move up."

"So what's the problem?"

"Letting go of you."

"What do you mean?"

"You're growing up. It's one thing to drive you to some track and sit on the infield and watch you run. But having you go away like this means you're going to be out of here someday. Soon."

Jamie laughed. "I have another year of high school. I'm not going anywhere."

Her dad put a hand on her shoulder. "Sweetheart, you're a rocket and your fuse is lit. It's only a matter of time before you blast off."

"What do I do?"

"Go talk to her."

Chapter 7
Family, Faith, and a Fast Car

TIM TOOK A WALK to the nearby convenience store. The only thing worse than listening to Tyson and Vera fight was listening to them fight while they brought groceries in from the truck. Vera didn't like Tyson opening stuff on the way home, and it always led to some kind of quarrel, so Tim tried to be gone when they got home.

At the store Tim bought a bottle of soda, a king-size Snickers bar, and a copy of *NASCAR Scene*. He sat on the sidewalk outside, flipping through the pages of race results, point standings, and pictures.

Toward the back, after the news about the top drivers, was a picture of Dale Maxwell standing by an old barn. In the background was a house—out of focus and fuzzy. He had his arm around his wife, a pretty woman with long red hair, and his kids, Kellen and Jamie, were beside them. Tim recognized Jamie from the Daytona coverage when she had taken over for a sick spotter.

"Family, Faith, and a Fast Car" was the title of the article. It detailed Dale Maxwell's current sponsor problems and described him as a "devoted husband and father first" and a NASCAR driver second.

That's probably why he's got sponsor problems, Tim thought. *He ought to put his racing first.*

"Some people say God and racing don't mix," Maxwell said. "I can't imagine climbing into the cockpit of a race car and not believing in God."

Great, Tim thought. *I'm moving in with a gang of Christians.*

The article went on to talk about Maxwell's record of "clean driving," his philosophy of racing ("When you cross the finish line first, act like you've been there before"), and his devotion to his kids. "Racing is a family affair with us. We've chosen to send the kids to a public school and let them have a 'normal life,' but we wouldn't do this if everybody didn't enjoy it. I'd rather flip burgers or change oil and have a close family life than win every race and lose my kids."

An old beater of a car pulled in to the gas station as Tim looked through the rest of the newspaper. He kept coming back to the Maxwell page. From traveling with his dad he'd known plenty of guys who were nice when you first met them but turned out to be snakes. Was this Maxwell guy just a good talker, or did he actually live the words he spoke?

"Guess I'll find out soon," Tim said out loud.

He was engrossed in his reading and didn't notice anyone behind him until the silhouette of someone's head blocked the light. He turned and saw three pairs of tennis shoes behind him. Tim looked up.

"Well, if it isn't the NASCAR janitor himself," Jeff said.

Chapter 8
Two Hearts

JAMIE'S MOM WAS HELPING Kellen fill out paperwork for an end-of-the-year field trip for his fifth grade class. Some Civil War battlefield or plantation or something. They had to complete everything early in order to go. Next fall he'd be in middle school, and Jamie thought her mom might be upset about all the changes the family was going through. If her mom would just hear her out, everything would be fine.

Her mom looked up, then studied the form closely. When she was done, she put it in Kellen's backpack, along with a check for the cost of the trip, and told him to brush his teeth and crawl into bed.

Jamie hovered around the door, not saying anything, believing her mom knew she wanted to talk. She followed her mom downstairs to the kitchen and watched her open a container of low-fat yogurt. She sat at the table, running a spoon around the top, stirring and staring.

"You always told us not to play with our food," Jamie said.

Her mom stifled a smile. "I remember when you were little. All I could get you to eat was cottage cheese and applesauce."

"I don't remember that."

"You were about two. I'd sit you in your booster seat at the table, and you wouldn't touch anything I put in front of you. And the applesauce always had to have cinnamon in it. You said you wanted some 'cimanon.' It was the cutest thing."

"Mom, about the driving school . . ."

Her mom stuck her spoon in the yogurt and left it there. "I've tried to let go of you a little at a time. Over the years I've allowed you to make decisions on your own. Letting you start racing was hard, even in the go-kart stage, because I knew you'd probably like it. But I gave in on that." She looked up. "But on this, Jamie, I've got to tell you that I have a bad feeling."

"Mom, you don't have to worry. I'll probably be the worst in the whole class."

"No," her mom said. "I know you'll do well. You have what it takes to do anything you set your mind to . . . except one thing."

"What's that?"

Her mom teared up and ran the spoon around the yogurt again. "A mother who has enough faith to give you to God and let him take over."

"Oh, Mom," Jamie said, and she could feel the emotion welling.

"It's true," her mother said. "I've prayed for you every day of your life and even before we knew we were going to have you. I prayed that God would protect you and give you a heart for him."

"You're probably disappointed."

"No. I know he's still working on you just like he is on me. And I've prayed about the man you're going to marry, and—"

"I hope you've prayed that he's cute."

They both laughed. Then her mother stood and embraced Jamie. "Life gives us a lot of twists and turns. Your father and I have had a number of those through the years. I want to protect you from making mistakes and getting hurt, but I know that's not going to be my job much longer. I'm having a hard time with this."

"Is it the schoolwork you're worried about? Because I can talk with my teachers, and I can do the rest of the semester on my own. Is that part of the problem?"

Her mom shook her head.

"Then if it's the money, I had a guy call tonight about my car. Selling that will give me enough for the room and board."

"Jamie, I don't expect you to understand this. . . ."

"You always say that right before you say something that's not fair."

"What do you want me to do? Just say you can go and not care?"

"I want you to say you believe in me and really mean it!" Jamie said. "To follow it with action. You've told me all my life to follow my dreams and dream big. I'm doing that, Mom, but now you're the one standing in my way. I thought it would be Dad, but it's you. What's up with that?"

Her mom stared at the spoon. "You're asking me to ignore what I feel in my gut, what I feel deep inside. I can't shut that down."

Jamie sank to a kitchen chair. "I don't want you to ignore your gut. I want you to believe in *my* gut."

"You haven't even thought this through."

"Mom, this is the kind of break I've been waiting for. Instead of racing in Dad's shadow, I can make a name for myself. I can learn from the best. I can follow my heart, like you've always said. Instead, you want me to follow your gut."

"You know that's not fair," her mom said. "You're using my words against me."

Jamie stood, her arms held up as if in a prayer. "I don't know what to do. I can't get you to see this. I'm still your little girl asking for cinnamon on my applesauce." She headed for the stairs.

"Jamie, don't leave."

"I can't talk, Mom. I'll say something I'll regret."

Chapter 9
Swamp Confession

TIM STRUGGLED AGAINST the three guys, but Jeff had seized his arms and held them behind his back. The other two grabbed his legs and carried him toward the old beater of a car.

Someone behind the counter at the store walked out and yelled at the guys, but one of them said, "He's a friend of ours. It's his birthday, and we're taking him to his party."

"It's not true!" Tim shouted. "Call the po—"

Jeff clamped a hand over his mouth and whispered in his ear, "If you want to survive this, you better keep your mouth shut."

He threw Tim in the backseat, and the other two sat on either side of him. Jeff started the car after a couple of tries—Tim listened to the engine and was pretty sure it needed a new head gasket and probably wouldn't last another 100 miles—and sped away from the store. They zoomed past Tyson's trailer, going too fast through the trailer park.

"You might want to slow down," Tim said. "Kids play in the street here all the time."

"Thanks, officer," Jeff said with a straight face, then broke into a laugh. "If kids are playing out here this time of night, they deserve to get hit."

Jeff's friends tightened their grip on Tim's arms as they drove past the playground and onto a gravel path. A sign said No Autos Allowed beyond This Point. Jeff turned on the radio to a country station, and the guys laughed loud and pretended to enjoy it, making fun of a song about a guy kissing girls and shooting squirrels.

The headlights illuminated a man and a woman walking on the path. The man waved his flashlight wildly, and the two had to jump into the weeds to avoid getting hit.

Jeff drove faster and slid to a stop in a hail of dust and gravel. They were at the pier of the lake. "Time to go for a swim, little buddy," he said.

Tim hated hearing those words coming from Jeff's mouth because his father had called him little buddy when Tim was young. He seethed, clenching his teeth as they pulled him from the backseat. As a kid, Tim had loved playing the Hulk. He'd turn into a strong, menacing character and win any battle single-handedly. He shut his eyes and tried to turn into the green monster, a maniac with rippling muscles. He didn't necessarily want to split his clothes—he just wanted to show these guys who was boss. Unfortunately it was a kid's game and only in his mind.

They easily dragged him to the railing of the pier, where couples in love usually stood to watch the sunset and kids threw pieces of bread to ducks who survived gator attacks. A sign by the overlook said Danger: No Swimming.

Jeff's friends held Tim against the railing and pushed his head toward the water.

Jeff put his face next to Tim's and spoke through clenched teeth. "You have no idea the trouble you caused me. I promised myself that if I ever found you again, I'd make you pay."

"You're the one who stole my tickets to Daytona," Tim said. "I'm the one who deserves to get payback."

"After what you did at that church?" Jeff yelled, jerking Tim's hair back so hard that Tim thought it would come out in clumps. "Do you know how much it cost to get my tooth fixed?"

It made Tim feel a little better that their scuffle in the church stairwell had cost Jeff something. But when he noticed a ripple in the water below and a greenish gray back floating on top, he tried to grab hold of the railing.

"After this, we're even," Jeff said. "You got it? You leave me alone and I'll leave you alone."

"How can we be even if you kill me?" Tim said.

"Not going to kill you, just going to let you get a little wet."

"I can't swim," Tim said.

The three laughed and pitched him over the railing.

Chapter 10
Autographed Car

JAMIE'S MOM AND DAD were talking in the kitchen early the next morning, sipping coffee and flipping the onionskin pages of Bibles. They did this every morning whether her dad was on the road or not. When he was at a race, they talked on the phone and prayed together. Part of Jamie liked that they were in love and made God the center of their lives. Another part of her felt it was schmaltzy, like some figurine of Jesus with his arm around a race car driver. She was sure their belief wasn't fake like some. Still, she didn't know if she could ever be that good.

Jamie paused on the stairs, looking through the door at her parents holding hands, their eyes closed, heads bowed. She wished they would find some verse in the Bible that said, "Thou shalt let thy daughter follow her NASCAR dream and not hinder her, for she wilt one day win the Nextel Cup," but she'd read enough of the Bible to know there was nothing like that in there. Although there was some verse about running a race so you could win the prize.

She slipped out of the house without facing them and hopped in Maxie, her restored 1965 Ford Mustang. She'd bought the car and worked on it for a solid year before getting her driver's license. It was almost a part of the family, and she hated the thought of selling it (though an ad had already run in the paper), but if she couldn't sell her Legend car, she'd have to sell Maxie. She needed the money.

She glanced at the house and saw her father's face in the kitchen window, then put the car in first and spun her tires in the gravel. Her mom stepped onto the porch in her bathrobe. Jamie was already halfway down the driveway, and she glanced in her rearview mirror and saw her mom wave.

Jamie went through the motions at school that day, not able to think of anything but the Skylar Jennings Driving School.

As usual, Cassie met her for lunch in the commons. "I heard from the prayer tree that Chad's doing a lot better and will probably come home today. They said he might have a pinched nerve in his neck or something that'll hurt for a while, but all the other blood work came out fine. Isn't that great?"

Jamie nodded. It was hard to think about Chad when her whole world was screeching to a halt.

"You don't seem very excited," Cassie said. "What's wrong?"

Jamie sighed. "How do you do that? Crawl inside my head and know what I'm thinking?"

"I don't know what you're thinking. That's why I asked you." Cassie opened her bagel sandwich and whispered a brief prayer.

Then Jamie spilled the story about why she felt so bad. "It's like I'm a mountain climber and I'm within a few feet of the top of Mount Everest, but somebody comes along and makes me climb down."

"Wait, let's look at the positives here," Cassie said.

"What could you possibly see as positive from all that?"

"Well, first, you are in the top 43 prospects in the country. I'd say that's pretty good. Plus, there's one of the top drivers in the world who's willing to put money behind you to send you to that school."

"Yeah, but what good does it do if that happens but I can't go?"

Cassie tried to get a piece of stuck bagel from her teeth. "From what I hear, storms whip up fast on Everest, and if you're not careful, you can fall to your death. Maybe that's what your mom is concerned about."

Jamie shook her head. "And that's supposed to encourage me?"

"Just shooting straight. But, Jamie, if I know your mom, she'll listen to your side. Show her you're serious. That you're ready."

"Like how?"

"Talk to some of your teachers. Get their permission to make up the work you're going to miss."

A light went on in her head. "And sell the race car to get enough money to pay for my room and board."

"There you go. Eliminate every one of her obstacles so she sees you're not only serious enough to talk about this, but you really want to do it. Make her have to say yes, you know?"

"Won't that make her mad? She already thinks I'm a disobedient daughter."

Cassie smiled. "You have a backbone, Jamie. She likes that and hates it at the same time. It means you're growing up."

By the time school ended, Jamie had talked with three of her teachers and the school guidance counselor. All the teachers frowned when she mentioned missing the last month of school.

"How do you make up PE?" her gym teacher said. "Explain how you can do that, and I'll get on board."

Her guidance counselor was more encouraging, but he was one of those people who always saw the gas tank half full. "If you want this enough and you're willing to work for it, the teachers can be persuaded. That's your job now." He got a glint in his eye and said, "I know I'm going to see you interviewed on TV one day, standing by your car, holding a trophy over your head. You need to come up with something interesting to do when you win—like that guy who used to jump off the top of his car backwards."

"I know who you mean," Jamie said.

"Maybe you could do some kind of dance on the hood. I think whatever it is, you should start practicing right now."

Jamie drove to her after-school job at the car-parts store. She helped stock the shelves and waited on customers at times, but mostly she drove the little white truck to garages and repair shops, delivering fuel pumps, brake parts, and whatever else the mechanics needed.

She'd checked her cell phone right after school and heard a message from her mom. "Just wanted to see how your day went. Call me when you get a chance."

Jamie made her final delivery just before six o'clock and headed home, still with the store hat and jacket on. She liked to think that someday this chain of stores would actually sponsor the car she drove, and her dad had even taken a few pictures of her at work so they could use them for a story about her past. She could imagine the headline in *Stock Car Racing*: "Delivery Girl Delivers the Cup to Sponsor."

When she got home, a strange truck and trailer were parked next to the barn, and a man was there talking to her mom.

"I didn't know you were Dale Maxwell's daughter," the man said, smiling. He introduced himself and shook hands. "Now that's a real good handshake you got there."

"My dad taught me never to hand anybody a dead fish."

The man laughed. "Hope you don't mind—I already looked at the car, even took it down the road a piece. You've obviously kept it in good shape."

"We had a mishap in Alabama in January, but Dad's team helped me repair the back end. It's a real good car. I hate to get rid of it."

"You said you were moving up," the man said. "To what?"

Jamie glanced at her mom. "I'm not exactly sure right now. But I need the money."

The man asked if she was firm on her asking price, and she said she might take a couple hundred less.

As he wrote out a check right there, Jamie took out her helmet and some tools she stored inside the car.

"Just for grins," the man said, "can you autograph the top right here?"

Jamie ran back inside to print out a bill of sale and brought a Sharpie with her. She signed the car in two places and on the back of the bill of sale.

The man shook hands with her again and drove away.

She looked at the check. It was for almost exactly the amount she'd need to pay her driving school bill. If she got to go.

Chapter 11
Missed Call

TIM STUMBLED INTO THE TRAILER, and Vera yelled at him. She had a way of stringing her sentences together like plugging extension cords into each other to make one long cord. "How did you get all wet? Where have you been, anyway? You're not tracking that mud and muck into my house. Get outside! I swear, I don't understand teenagers!"

Tim felt glad to be alive, and Vera was worried about her precious linoleum. It felt kind of like she was rearranging the pictures on the *Titanic*'s walls. The ship was going down, but she was focused on the tiny stuff.

He stepped outside, took off his shoes, and squeezed the water out of his socks. He thought she might bring him a towel or something, but she didn't.

Tim just stood out there, and he could tell people in the next trailer were watching.

He shivered, not because of the cold but because of the way the gator had splashed when he'd gone into the water. He'd heard they were hungry in the evening and would eat anything thrown at them—a chicken or a basketball—it didn't matter. So when he hit the water, he flailed for the pier posts and grabbed them. He couldn't swim—that part of what he'd said had been true—but he tried to hold his breath so he would float. His dad had told him that much. He didn't give the gators time to bite at him—he'd shinnied up the pole and listened for the car to pull away, then climbed onto the pier and walked home.

He paused at the front door and heard Vera and Tyson fighting over the noise of the TV. Funny how money was too tight to afford new clothes for Tim, but they'd been able to buy a satellite dish with a bunch of premium channels.

Tim opened the door and crept to his room, but Vera said something to him from the kitchen. He walked back to her and asked what she had said.

Vera had a thing about boxes—she had to take all the food out of them and put boxes in the trash before she felt done. She even took the cereal out of the boxes and left the plastic bags on the shelf so you never could tell what you were getting.

"Somebody called for you while you were gone. Where'd you go anyway?"

"Out for a walk. Who was it?"

"A guy. Had kind of a deep voice. Sounded like he was from up north."

"Did he say his name or anything?"

"No, just said he'd call back tomorrow."

Tim went back to his room, shut the door, and sat on the bed next to his ratty suitcase. He pulled out the lawyer's letter and the key. He didn't care how he got there or what the people were like; he had to get to North Carolina.

Chapter 12
The Bounce

JAMIE'S MOM AND DAD whispered a lot that night, but for the most part, Jamie stayed in her room and finished her homework, then started on a letter to her teachers. She had to convince them (and her mom) that finishing the year on her own would be a good idea. Even if she had to repeat the semester, she was determined to get to the driving school.

Her dad was up early the next morning getting ready to leave for the race in Texas. There were more whispers and phone calls, but she tried to ignore them. One phone call did startle her—it was from her dad's main sponsor, and he went into the den he used for an office and closed the door. When he came back out, Jamie moved to the handrail at the top of the stairs and watched her dad hug her mom.

"It's gonna work out for the best—you know that," he said, kissing her mom on the head.

"Why are they putting so much pressure on you?" her mother said.

"They want a return on their investment, and I can't blame them."

"Things will come together this weekend," her mom said. "You've always done well at Texas. And Phoenix is next week."

"Let's hope we can wow them. You'll FedEx the tickets to Florida today, right?"

"I got it covered. We'll be watching and praying for you."

Without looking up, her dad said, "See you Sunday night, Jamie."

She waved and gave a halfhearted, "Bye."

Then he was out the door.

/////

Jamie handed the letter she had written to each teacher, but most of them didn't have a chance to read it before class.

Her English teacher, who had admitted she didn't know a thing about NASCAR other than how dangerous it was, scratched her chin and let her glasses ride down on her nose as she read the letter after class.

She called Jamie up. "This is a well-written letter, Jamie. If I were giving you a grade, I'd give you a C for grammar—" she pointed out two subject-verb agreement mistakes—"and an A for persuasion. You really want to do this."

"It's a huge opportunity, ma'am. It's hard to get noticed and break into the teams, and this could be my best shot."

"If you can convince your other teachers, I'll go along with it."

A ray of hope, a beam of sunlight, broke through the clouds.

But the storm came after school on her way to her job. Her mother called. "Jamie, I just got back from the store, and there's an urgent message here from the bank. You need to call a Mr. Conway right away."

She was passing the bank and pulled into the parking lot. It was a small brick building with the American and North Carolina flags flying out front. The lobby was always warm and inviting, and the lady at the front desk smiled like she was advertising a new toothpaste. Fresh-baked cookies sat on a tray, and the woman encouraged Jamie to take one.

"Thank you," Jamie said. "I'm looking for Mr. Conway."

"That's his office right there," the woman said. "Have a seat and I'll call him. Is he expecting you?"

Jamie told her he'd called her house, then sat and ate the chocolate chip cookie. It was about as big as her hand and tasted so sweet she knew she'd have to work extra hard at the fitness center tonight. She usually worked out twice a week to stay in shape and keep toned for her races.

"Miss Maxwell, come right in," Mr. Conway said. He was a middle-aged man, dressed in a black suit and a yellow tie. He had a nice smile, but his demeanor was all business.

"My mom called and said you left a message at the house."

He offered her a seat and sat behind his desk. "Yes. Something unfortunate has happened with a transaction." He picked up a check with a big red mark on it. "This check you cashed for a substantial amount of money was sent back to us for insufficient funds."

Jamie stared at the check. It was her car money. She'd deposited it the next day. "That's the check I got for selling my car."

"Well, there wasn't enough money in this person's account to cover that purchase." Mr. Conway looked at the floor and bit his lip. "What we usually tell our clients about selling expensive items like your car is that they should never take a personal check. Only a money order or a certified check."

"Maybe he made a mistake—maybe the money's there now."

"We sent the check through twice, and both times it came back. I'm very sorry, Miss Maxwell."

Jamie took a photocopy of the check and studied the man's name, address, and phone number. Now she had no money for the driving school. What else could go wrong?

Chapter 13
The Letter

TIM DIDN'T WANT TO GO TO SCHOOL. It made no sense for him to go when he was leaving, but Tyson and Vera made him. He went to the office after the first bell and told them that he was being sent to another state.

"Your parents will need to fill out and sign these forms," the secretary said, giving him a couple of papers. "You can hand them in to the counselor's office just down the hall."

Tim took the forms to the library, filled them out, then signed Tyson's and Vera's names. He took them to the right office and found an older lady at the desk. "I'm here to officially resign or whatever you call it."

"You're not dropping out, are you?" the woman said, her face creasing with concern.

"No, I'm moving up north. I just don't know what you call it."

"It's a withdrawal. Why aren't your guardians here to complete the process?"

Because they don't care enough to be, Tim thought. Instead he said, "They're kind of busy. You know, with all the business stuff they're doing."

She took the papers into the next room and came back with a signed yellow sheet that was his official ticket out. "Here you are. And good luck in your new home."

/////

Vera said they'd received a call from the family in North Carolina, and she told Tim to be ready the next day, though she wouldn't say much else. He slept late the next morning until he heard a vehicle with squeaky brakes stop outside the trailer. He'd slept in his clothes so he could be ready as fast as possible, and he went to the front room and looked out the window. It was a white FedEx truck, something he'd never seen in this neighborhood.

He stepped to the door, where a lady in a gray outfit waited.

"You Tim Carhardt?" she said.

"Yes, ma'am."

She scanned the bar code on the thin packet, handed it to him, and ran back to her truck. "Have a nice day!" she called over her shoulder.

"You too," he said.

Tim went back to his room and sat on the bed. At the top was a tab that said *Pull here*, and he pulled it across and opened the pack. Inside was a white envelope with *Tim Carhardt* written on the front. He opened the envelope and took out several pages and something printed on thicker paper that looked like tickets. Along with them was a handwritten page on stationery with *Nicole Maxwell* printed at the top. At the bottom was an address in Velocity, NC.

Dear Tim,

I'm so sorry for the delay in getting you here. Our family is excited about having you live with us, and we can't wait to help you get settled into your new room.

I talked with Tyson and Vera about this and hope they've told you our plans, but since Dale didn't get to drive you back up here, he thought you might enjoy the race in Texas this weekend. You'll find a plane ticket for this afternoon, and then you and Dale will fly back Sunday evening. He thought it would *be a good chance for you to get to know each other.*

I can't tell you how thrilled I am to meet you and have you join our family. We're all thinking of you and hoping your trip from Florida goes well.

See you soon!

Nicole

Tim read the letter twice before he folded it and examined the plane ticket. There were so many numbers on the thing that he couldn't figure it out. He finally saw the departure time from the Tallahassee airport: 06:55 p.m.

His heart raced. He'd never flown in an airplane before, and he'd heard horror stories about how long it took to get through security and that you couldn't bring any kind of liquids or things that could be used as a weapon.

Then something ran through him that he hadn't felt in a long time. Hope. Excitement. He was actually going to another race. Maybe he'd get to be down on pit road with the teams.

He pulled out the letter and read it again.

Chapter 14
Surprise Visitor

JAMIE RUBBED HER PALMS together, a nervous habit she had when she was stressed out.

"Have you told your mom about the bounced check?" Cassie asked.

They were at the youth group meeting at church but had gone into the little prayer room on the second floor. It had a chapel feel to it with stained glass in the windows and a cross on the wall. There were only a few chairs and a kneeling bench at the front.

"She asked what it was about, but I can't tell her," Jamie said. "It'll be the last nail in the coffin of the driving school. Instead of giving her every reason to say yes, I'm giving her every reason to say no."

"That guy who bought your car is a jerk," Cassie said. "I hate to say it, but it's true."

"But he seemed so nice."

"Did you call him yet?"

"Haven't got up the nerve. I thought about hiring a couple of the guys from the football team to go over there with me and act like mob hit men."

"Gary would be pretty intimidating. Or Trace, except he's kind of like a teddy bear."

"I can't believe that guy would stiff me for the money. He even got me to autograph the car."

"Some people are just that way," Cassie said. "Okay, I'm going to ask you something, and you have to promise me you won't take it the wrong way or get angry or anything like that."

Jamie furrowed her brow. "What is it?"

"Have you prayed about this? Now don't give me that look. I mean, have you really, honestly asked God to take control—not just of the car thing and the driving school but of your life? the whole thing?"

Jamie sighed. "Look, I'm never going to be a spiritual giant like you are—"

"Stop it. That's not fair. God doesn't love me any more than he loves you. And I'm not a spiritual giant—I mess up all the time."

"That's good to hear. What do you do, say a bad word every two years?"

"I'm not here to preach. I just think it would be a load off you if you asked God what he wants for you."

"I believe God wants us to take care of some things ourselves. He's busy, you know? Wars and people starving and global warming. He doesn't have time for some girl in North Carolina with NASCAR dreams."

"That's not true. He cares about every detail of your life."

"How could he, Cassie? Think of everybody in the world with a million problems each. How could he care for all that? It would drive him crazy."

"You're making God out to be like you and me, but he's not," Cassie said. "He's totally different. He wants to be a part of every decision you make."

"I think God wants us to work out our own lives," Jamie said. "Instead of running to him every time I have a problem or a choice of gum flavor or whether to have baloney or peanut-butter-and-jelly sandwiches, I think he wants us to choose the little stuff and bring just the big stuff to him."

"You got a verse for that?" Cassie said. "Because I have a boatload of stuff that talks about him being interested in all our needs."

"I'm sure you do. You know the Bible a lot better than I do, so it wouldn't be a fair match."

"How about, 'Give all your worries and cares to God, for he cares about you'? He doesn't say, 'Give the big worries you have to God' or 'Just give the cares that are important to God.' He says to give them *all* to him. Do you think Jesus acted like that?" Cassie put on her best Jesus face, the one that made her look perfect and half asleep. "'No, get those children out of here. I'm doing important things today like praying and meditating.'"

Jamie had to laugh.

"Jesus told his disciples to let the children come to him—he wasn't this busy guy who didn't have time for people. And God isn't like that either."

Jamie rubbed her palms and shifted in her chair. *There's no clock in here. How can there be no clock in here?*

"What are you thinking?" Cassie said.

Jamie sighed. "Okay, you want the truth? Maybe I'm scared of what God will think of the whole racing thing."

"What do you mean?"

"What if I do like you say and give my life to God and let him take control of my gum and which outfit to wear and what kind of gas to buy. The whole thing. What happens if he tells me he wants me to go to some foreign country where they don't even have cars, let alone racetracks? What then?"

"Two answers," Cassie said. "One—if you could know right now what God wants you to do with your life, what would please him most and bring glory to him, wouldn't you want to do that?"

"I don't know."

"Well, I think God offers the very best and most fulfilling life. I'd jump at the chance to know what he wants me to do."

"Good for you."

"Two—God doesn't usually do that. He doesn't write in the clouds or speak in a deep voice and tell you exactly what to do. But he does create a desire and interest in each of us, and he uses those things. Like your racing. Man, Jamie, it almost feels like you were born to get in a car and go fast. I think God can use that. Haven't you ever seen that movie *Chariots of Fire*?"

"I've heard about it."

"The guy's sister thought he should be a missionary and give up running. He told her, 'I believe God made me for a purpose, but he also made me fast. And when I run I feel his pleasure.'"

"You sure he didn't drive NASCAR?"

Cassie laughed. "The point is, God's not up there trying to take away what you love doing. He doesn't want to make you miserable. You can trust him with your life."

Someone knocked on the door. It was Pastor Gordon. "You two having fun in here?"

"Sorry," Cassie said. "Jamie's kind of having a little crisis, and we were talking about it."

"Crisis? I'd like to hear about that, but I thought you'd want to know there's somebody here to see you."

Chad Devalon stepped around the pastor and sheepishly waved.

"Chad!" Jamie said. She rushed to him and almost gave him a hug but thought better of it.

Pastor Gordon excused himself and walked down the hall.

"Your mom said you were over here," Chad said. He handed Jamie a colorful packet with the name *Skylar Jennings* on the front. "Dad wanted me to give this to you."

"Thanks," Jamie said.

"How are you feeling?" Cassie said.

"Doctor said I pinched something in my neck when I flipped. I'm kind of sore, but I'll be fine. Can't say the same about my car, but Dad said he would get me a new one."

Jamie couldn't help looking at the folder in her hands, and Chad picked up on it. He cleared his throat. "You probably know what that is by now. Guess you'll be seeing some of my friends at that school."

"You're not going?" Jamie said.

"They're inviting the top prospects, and I'm not a prospect anymore." He looked at the prayer room and made a face, rubbing his neck. "I gotta be going.

Can't say I've spent much time in churches. They give me the creeps."

"You should come to our youth group," Cassie said.

"Yeah, it's so good you two don't even go." Chad smiled. "I'll see you."

When Chad was gone, Jamie turned back to Cassie. "That runner in the movie. What happened to him?"

"He won an Olympic gold medal."

"What about after that?"

"He actually became a missionary and went to China . . . and died there."

Jamie stared at her. "Not a good ending to your story, Cassie."

Chapter 15
First Flight

TIM PACED OUTSIDE the trailer, waiting for Tyson to get back from work. He would rather have anyone drive him to the airport than Tyson because the guy was always late, but a little after five Tyson pulled up in the truck.

Tim rode in the backseat with his suitcase, checking the zippered front every few minutes to make sure the ticket was in there. He was nervous.

"It's not that big of a deal," Tyson said, glancing in the rearview mirror at Tim. "You just sit down, strap on the seat belt, and pray that metal tube doesn't fall out of the sky. I knew a guy who went down in a crash. Real shame. They sure didn't have an open casket for him."

Vera gave him a stern look, and Tyson shrugged. "What did I say? I'm telling him the truth. He oughta know stuff like that can happen."

Vera turned in her seat. "Tim, you have to prepare yourself for life up there in North Carolina. It's going to be a lot different. Those people probably aren't as nice as we are, and if they have their own kids, they're not going to pay much attention to you. So just be warned."

"Thanks," Tim said. *I wonder if they'll put labels on their food.*

When they arrived at the regional airport, Tim grabbed his suitcase and jumped out.

Vera rolled her window down to say good-bye, but Tyson actually got out and pointed to the door Tim would enter and the counter inside where he'd check in.

"Come on, Tyson. I want to beat the dinner rush at the Golden Corral," Vera said.

Tyson shook Tim's hand. "Good knowin' you. Have a nice life, buddy."

Tim walked inside and stood in line until it was his turn. He handed over his ticket, and the man asked if he wanted to check his baggage.

"I checked it already," Tim said. "I put some duct tape on the inside so it wouldn't come open. I think it'll be okay."

"No, son, checking means you give me your suitcase, and I put it on the plane for you. Do you want to check it or carry it on with you?"

"Oh," Tim said. "Well, does it cost any more to have you take it?"

"No," the man said, weighing the bag.

"But how do I get it back when I get to Dallas?"

"We'll take care of that," the man said. "Just go to baggage claim when you get there."

Baggage claim, Tim thought, trying to remember the words.

The man put the bag on a conveyor belt behind him and asked Tim for some ID.

Tim handed him his high school ID, and the man asked how old he was. It was right then that Tim wished he could have taken a bus.

"Are you traveling with your parents?" the man said.

"No, sir."

"Well, since you're 15, you're an unaccompanied minor. Are you okay making the connection in Houston? You have to change planes there."

Tim swallowed hard. "I guess I'm okay with it."

The man pointed out the security area and told Tim where he'd find his gate. They made him take off his shoes and walk through a metal detector, and it went off. Tim had forgotten to pack his pocketknife in his suitcase, the one his dad had given him.

"You can't take this on the plane," a tall man said.

"What do I do with it?"

"You have to leave it here."

"How do I get it back?"

"We could mail it to you."

Tim couldn't think of the Maxwells' address, and people behind him were giving him mean stares. "That's okay. You can just throw it out."

A half hour before the plane was scheduled to leave, a lady at the gate got on a microphone and gave instructions for people not to crowd onto the plane, but it didn't do any good because they pushed and got in line anyway. It was like a high school cafeteria.

When Tim got to the door of the plane, the lady put his ticket through a machine, and he went down the Jetway. His seat was 15A, but he couldn't figure out where the numbers were on the seats, and by the time he was a few rows back, he couldn't count. He guessed and sat down. A few minutes later a guy said he was in his seat, and the flight attendant came and showed Tim row 15.

Lifting off made his stomach lurch, but he was glad he was sitting next to the window because he liked seeing the ground rather than not seeing it. Tyson's words came back, and he imagined the plane falling from the sky. If the plane went down, he wanted to land on Jeff's house.

/////

The Dallas airport was laid out a lot better than the one in Houston. Instead of walking a mile or two to figure out where he was going, Tim found the baggage claim not very far away. He followed the other passengers—many of whom were wearing NASCAR hats and shirts—into a glass-enclosed area with big conveyor belts that ran around the room.

As soon as he walked in, he saw a guy holding a big poster board over his head with *Tim Carhardt* written on it in big letters. Dale Maxwell didn't look much like a race car driver standing in the middle of all these people, but Tim recognized his face even before reading the sign. He walked up to him.

The man smiled, put the poster down, and held out his hand. "Tim, it's nice to meet you. I'm Dale Maxwell."

"I know who you are," Tim said, shaking his hand and looking at the floor. The guy had a nice pair of boots—that was for sure. "I thought you'd send somebody else to pick me up."

"Wouldn't trust this job to anyone else," Mr. Maxwell said. "How was the flight?"

"Okay, I guess. I don't have much to compare it to."

"Your first?"

"Yeah. They took my pocketknife back in Tallahassee."

"Couldn't you have given it to Tyson?"

"He and Vera didn't go in with me."

Tim looked up to see Mr. Maxwell's face get kind of tight, like somebody was trying to pass him on the outside in turn one. Actually, it looked like he wanted to say a bad word.

"I'm really sorry about that, Tim. I talked with Tyson, and he said he would walk you all the way to your gate. Was there anyone in Houston to help you change planes?"

"No, but I made it okay."

Mr. Maxwell studied the baggage carousel and pursed his lips. "Was it a special knife?"

"Just one my dad gave me."

The conveyor belt started, and they moved toward it. Tim's suitcase came out, and he'd been wrong about the duct tape. The side was split, and his underwear was sticking out. He shoved it back inside and held it together while he headed toward the door with Mr. Maxwell.

"Let me take that for you," Mr. Maxwell said.

"No, I got it."

When they walked outside, Tim relaxed a little. He was glad he didn't have to find his way around by himself and could just follow this guy to his car. It was parked pretty close. Mr. Maxwell opened the trunk of the rental, and Tim threw his suitcase inside.

They stopped to pay for parking, and then Mr. Maxwell told him they'd be staying at a hotel close to the track.

"That big one that sits right on turn two?"

"No, that's not a hotel. That has offices and condominiums. Pretty pricey. But the place we'll stay is nice."

Tim didn't know what to say next or if he should say anything, and there were a few minutes of awkward silence until Mr. Maxwell turned on the radio.

Finally Tim got up the nerve to speak. "Sir, I don't know what to call you."

"Well, if you were a little kid, I'd have you call me Mr. Maxwell, but to be honest, Mr. Maxwell is my dad. My name's Dale. I think that's as good as anything. Unless you feel better calling me Your Highness. A couple of drivers have called me some names I can't repeat. I'd rather you didn't call me any of those."

Tim smiled.

"So is Dale okay with you?"

"Yeah. And you can call me Tim."

"Deal." They drove a few miles before Dale said, "You attached to that suitcase in the back? It doesn't have any sentimental value to you, does it?"

"No, it's just something Vera said I could have."

Dale took the next exit and made a few turns into a Wal-Mart parking lot. They walked back to the section that had luggage, and Dale picked out what looked to Tim like the biggest suitcase in the history of travel.

"Think this will work?"

Tim nodded. "You could probably fit Vera's entire kitchen in there twice," he said as he pulled it to the checkout.

"You're going to need the extra room after this weekend," Dale said.

"What do you mean?"

"Well, if that's all the clothes you have, we need to get you outfitted before you leave."

They stood in a line four deep at the express checkout.

A kid about eight years old stopped and stared at Dale. His jaw dropped and so did the wallet he was holding. The family with him walked on while the kid stood there.

"Is there something wrong, son?" Dale said.

"Y-y-you're Dale Maxwell, aren't you?"

Dale smiled. "That's me. You going to the race Sunday?"

"No, but I'm going to watch it on TV." The kid turned and yelled for his dad. By now a crowd was forming, and two women fumbled with their purses to find paper for an autograph.

Dale swiped his credit card for the suitcase, then signed autographs as people huddled around him.

An older woman pushed through and had Dale sign her address book. "I thank you kindly," she said. "You know, I think you're the cleanest driver out there. But just once I'd like to see you cut that Butch Devalon off and slam him into the wall."

Dale grinned. "Well, don't think I haven't thought about doing that same thing a time or two."

"I don't expect you will, but I swear I'd like to see it."

The kid came back with a shirt and a hat, and Dale signed them with a Sharpie the cashier loaned him. "Good luck, Mr. Maxwell, sir," the kid said as they finally got away.

Tim turned back, and the kid looked like he'd just seen Santa Claus or Elvis or maybe Elvis dressed as Santa Claus. He held up his shirt and beamed at his father. "Can you believe it? We met Dale Maxwell in Wal-Mart!"

"He's not as tall as I thought he'd be," someone said.

When they got to the car, Dale opened the old suitcase and helped Tim transfer his stuff into the new one. Then he took the old, ratty suitcase with the duct tape and stuffed it in a trash can at the end of the parking lot.

"Does that happen a lot?" Tim said. "People coming up for autographs?"

"Happens more on the road than at home. People back there are used to seeing drivers and crew members at the store. Everybody's got to get groceries, you know?"

Chapter 16
Facing Sparky

JAMIE SAT IN MAXIE with the ignition off, the packet Chad had given her on the seat next to her, staring through the fog at the farm. She hadn't slept much the night before, and if she didn't hurry, she'd be late for work. She watched for any sign of movement on the farm, but all was quiet except for a big black dog that came near the road and barked at her, then went back to the front porch.

Her Legend car sat on the hauling trailer beside the barn. Her stomach rumbled, and it was as much from hunger as it was from her nerves. She banged the steering wheel and shook her head. The phrase from the letter inside the packet came back to her: *unless the amount is paid in full before the course begins . . .*

She'd tried to think of any way out of doing what she had to do, but in the end she knew she'd have to face the man herself. Her mom would say that if she couldn't even deal with the guy who'd written the bad check, how was she going to handle the world of NASCAR? Of course, sitting behind the steering wheel and holding off other drivers was a lot different from this.

"Come on," she said softly to herself. "Be a man. Or at least a really strong woman."

She smiled. Cassie had called last night and said she'd pray for her. She wondered if that meant Cassie was getting up this early on a Saturday or if she just slipped in a quick prayer before she went to bed.

"Okay, let's do this," Jamie said aloud to snap herself awake. She started the car and pulled it into the driveway, then slammed her door so whoever was inside would hear someone was there.

She didn't have to worry about that because the dog took care of it. He came bounding down the stairs barking and snarling and showing his teeth. She tried to soothe him with her voice, but he wasn't having any of it. The hair on his back stood straight up, his eyes looked red—like some kind of Satan dog—and his mouth was about as wide as I-77.

"Sparky, get back here!" a woman yelled from the door.

Sparky? Jamie thought. The name didn't fit the woof at all.

"Can I help you?" the woman said.

Jamie tried to talk over the noise of the dog, but every time she spoke, Sparky barked louder and inched closer, and the white stuff in the corners of his mouth hung down. She could see his rib cage and the bones of his hips, and he looked like he needed a good meal. She figured that's exactly what she seemed like to him.

"Can I come in there?" Jamie shouted.

The woman nodded and opened the door. Jamie sidestepped Sparky and made it into the house, and the woman closed the door. "He wouldn't hurt you. He's just hungry for breakfast. What can I do for you?"

The house smelled like Jamie's grandmother's place. Lots of old wood and linoleum. The boards creaked in the front room when she took a step. And it was hot inside—about 10 degrees warmer than it needed to be.

The man who had given her the bad check stomped downstairs, stretching into a work jacket. When he saw her, his steps slowed.

"I need a word with you, sir," Jamie said.

"This is the Maxwell girl, dear," the man said when he reached the bottom step.

"The racer's daughter?" the woman said.

"More than a daughter—she's a racer too. And

a good one, I hear. Now you're not wanting that car back, are you? Because my grandson has his heart set on driving it this afternoon. He's sure excited."

"I'm glad," Jamie said, pulling the copy of his check out of her pocket. "But I've got a problem. I went to cash this, and they said there were insufficient funds."

He took it and held it at arm's length. "How in the world? There must be some mistake. . . . Oh, I know. The mortgage payment probably came at the same time. I'll go write you another one. There shouldn't be a problem now." He moved to the kitchen and took out his checkbook.

Jamie cleared her throat. "If it wouldn't be too much trouble, do you think we could go down to the bank and get a cashier's check or a certified check?"

He turned and his face went a little white. "Now that won't be necessary, Jamie. I'm sorry for your trouble, but it was an honest mistake."

Jamie glanced out the front window. Sparky was looking in at her. "I believe that. I'm sure you didn't mean to do this, but I can't afford to pay for another bounced check."

"Well, that's what I'm saying. This one won't bounce. I'll write you another one right now, and you can be on your way."

Jamie locked eyes with him and tried to calm the

butterflies in her stomach. "Mister, I'm only 16. I don't know a lot about selling cars and doing business, but a guy at the bank said I should never take a personal check for something this expensive. If you don't have the money, I can call a friend and come out here and get the car. But I have to either have the money or the car."

The man looked at his watch. "I'm late to work as it is."

"If I don't get paid for that car, there's no way I can get into a school that I want to attend. So if you don't have it, let me take it and sell it to somebody else." Her teeth were chattering like global cooling had begun.

The woman stepped into the shadows of the front room and turned to her husband. "Go down to the bank and make this right. This girl had to drive all the way out here."

His voice became meaner. "I told you—I have to get to work."

Jamie let the two look at each other.

Finally the man sighed and shook his head. "All right. Get in your car and follow me down to the bank."

Chapter 17
Race Prep

TIM WOKE UP LATE and couldn't remember where he was. The bed he was in had a big white comforter that was thicker than he was. *Hotel,* he thought. The big one near the speedway in Fort Worth. But where was Dale? He got up and walked through the suite. He had been sleeping in one room while Dale slept in the other. He opened the curtains, and the Texas sun blasted the room. He saw the speedway in the distance and a sea of colorful cars, RVs, and haulers. He wondered how much a room here cost on race weekend.

He closed the curtains and headed for the bathroom but stopped at Dale's bed. On the nightstand was an open black book, and Tim hovered over it, not turning any pages, just looking. It was a Bible, and beside it was a leather notebook with scribbling in it. He couldn't read the writing very well, but it looked like personal stuff and what God was teaching him and junk like that. At the bottom were the initials *P.R.* Under that were three names: *Chad, Jamie, Tim.*

He couldn't figure that one out, so he turned toward the bathroom and saw a piece of paper taped to the front of the TV. *This guy knows me pretty good already*, he thought. *Just like Vera taping notes on the food in the fridge.*

Tim,

I headed over to the track early for a practice session and a drivers' meeting. You were sleeping soundly, so I didn't want to wake you. As I told you last night, I've asked Scotty to call you so you two can grab something to eat and then come over to the track. If you want to stay in the room, that's fine too. Just tell Scotty.

Whatever you decide, I'll see you soon.

Dale

These people sure like to write a lot of notes, Tim thought.

He took a shower and got dressed, and as he was coming out of the bathroom, the phone rang.

Scotty was a little shorter than Dale and had what Tim thought was a round, kind face. He had a good tan, which was usual for people who stood on top of buildings during summer Sundays and watched car races. They met in the lobby, and Scotty took Tim into a restaurant and said he could order whatever he wanted. He chose the buffet, which had just about everything a guy would want for breakfast and then some.

"If I eat one more bite, I'm going to pop," Tim said when he'd finished his second plate.

Scotty shoved his plate away and drained the last of his orange juice. "So, how do you feel about Dale and his family having you come to stay with them?"

"I haven't met the family, but so far Dale seems okay."

Scotty leaned forward, elbows on the table, his fingers interlaced. "Dale takes his family seriously. He'd shoot me if he knew I was saying this, but there's some stuff I think you should know."

"Go ahead," Tim said.

"I know you've had it rough. And everybody wants you to find a good home. But Dale doesn't drive as well when his personal life is messed up."

"You think I'm going to mess up his life?"

"Not on purpose. But there's something going on with his daughter that has him distracted. In the past, if he and his wife had a fight or a disagreement, those of us on the team could see that. It's hard enough to drive out there with no distractions, but stuff at home affects him, and if it affects *him*, it affects *us*. The team depends on him."

"I know how it works."

Scotty held up his hands. "I know you're not new to the business, and I'm real sorry about your—"

"You want me to go back to Florida? Is that it?"

"No, not at all. In fact, having you here might even help things. I don't have any idea. But there's a lot of talk about the sponsor and the future of Dale's career."

"I'm not going to cause trouble."

"I know. I probably shouldn't have even brought this up. None of what's happened is your fault."

"It's good to know what's going on. I won't mess anything up. I promise."

"There's one more thing," Scotty said. "If you haven't picked up on it already, Dale's pretty religious. He's not pushy, for the most part, but he doesn't like bad language, and he's probably blocked access to any movies in your room."

"I don't have a problem with religious people as long as they leave me alone."

"Well, good luck living with him and his wife."

Scotty gave Tim his credentials—a child's pass and the lanyard, the fancy plastic thing to wear around his neck. He'd have to keep that on at all times while at the track. He also knew he couldn't wear sandals and shorts there, even though that would be a lot cooler than jeans and tennis shoes. It was a safety precaution.

They took the shuttle across Highway 114 and walked to the entrance where drivers and their teams were checked in.

The Texas track was a 1.5 mile oval and could handle both stock car and Indy type racers. Tim figured Dale liked it because the banking in the turns was the same as the track in Charlotte—24 degrees. Talladega and Daytona had some of the steepest turns.

Scotty took Tim directly to the hauler to meet the rest of the team, passing the long garage that was a beehive of activity. People with garage and pit passes milled about with their cameras, looking at cars and keeping an eye out for a driver or a familiar crew chief.

They passed the Devalon hauler with the crash cart and pit box out front as well as their frame tents set up to keep people in the shade. The sun baked everything here, especially the track, so the team had to adjust to the extreme temperatures. With the

Devalon team, everything sparkled, including the crew's uniforms.

The Maxwell hauler was parked at the far end of the track, and though it was clean, it was clear it wasn't in the same league as Devalon's and some others.

A tall guy with spiky hair and a day's growth of beard was outside looking at their tires. Tim could tell as soon as he saw him that this was their jackman. The guy who lugged the jack to either side of the car was usually the strongest and quickest on the crew.

"Tim, this is Cal," Scotty said.

Cal shook his hand and said he was glad to meet him. "I've seen you at a couple of races before. Your dad was good at what he did. We all miss him."

Tim nodded.

"Where's T.J.?" Scotty said.

"Over at the track. Dale's still in his practice run before qualifying. Having trouble getting the wedge right."

Scotty introduced Tim to the other crew members, then turned and lowered his voice. "I have to warn you about Mac. He's a little territorial."

"Is he your hauler driver?" Tim said. "My dad knew him. Said he was kind of cranky."

"That's a nice way of saying it. A better way would be to say he's a mad old dog who'll bark at you for no reason and bite for less."

"If he's so mean, why does Dale keep him on the team?"

"That's a good question. Guess you'll have to ask Dale that."

They walked toward the pit, and Tim put in his earplugs. He'd been around the tracks long enough to be able to stand the noise without them, but it was a lot easier blocking it out.

Scotty pointed to the track and Dale's car as it sped past the start line. Tim followed him into the back straightaway until he lost sight of the car in the line of RVs and haulers. Out of the fourth turn the car shifted a little.

"Looks like it's loose in the turn," Tim said.

Scotty nodded. "He's gonna have to bring it in."

They headed over to pit road as Dale drove in. The rear tire carrier turned the tool in the back, adjusting the rear jack bolt so it would hold better in the turn. They always ran the risk of making it too tight or too loose.

Scotty grabbed two headsets and let Tim listen as Dale roared out of the pits and back onto the track. The crew chief waved at them and gave them a thumbs-up as they climbed onto the pit box.

Tim examined the video monitors and equipment. The setup wasn't as fancy as Devalon's, but it worked. From up here, Tim could see almost the entire track. He watched Dale take turn two, accelerate down the backstretch, and hit the groove on the third and fourth turns.

"Oh yeah," Dale said. "That's a lot better. T.J., looks like we got us a car this weekend."

"I got a real good feeling about it, Dale."

The Maxwell team drew 33rd position to qualify. As the track got hotter, the times were faster, so it was to their advantage to go as close to the end as they could. Tim stayed up on the pit box to watch as car after car took their two laps around the track. The fastest lap counted.

Fans filled about half the stands—some there to watch the qualifying, some early for the truck race—and cheered when their favorite drivers entered the track. Butch Devalon's time was 28.772 seconds, good enough for pole position when he finished, but there were still a lot of cars waiting.

Dale was out of his car, talking to T.J., laughing, and smacking the top of the car.

Tim looked around at the different teams, the excitement level rising this day before the race. *Wish you were here, Dad,* he thought.

Dale entered the track and ran through the back turns, then took the green flag. His brakes lit as he entered the first turn, following the groove of the track. His front end slipped a little as the car hit the straightaway.

The crew chief keyed his microphone. "That's gonna cost you—let's get a good second lap."

"Hit some loose stuff on turn two," Dale said. "Here we go."

"Engine sounds good," Tim said to Scotty, lifting one headphone. "Really tight."

Scotty nodded.

When Dale crossed the start/finish line the first time, his time was 29.024. Not bad, but if he wanted to be close to the front at the start, he'd have to do better.

Tim stood as Dale passed the second time. He held it in turn two, and the engine roared down the backstretch. He shot out of turn four and screamed toward the checkered flag. Tim looked up to the scoring pylon to see Dale's car, #14, in first place with a time of 27.859 at a speed of 193.833 mph.

"Woo-hoo!" T.J. yelled. "You've got the pole right now, Dale. Good work."

As it turned out, Dale wound up in the ninth position with the top car qualifying at just over 27 seconds. Still, the crew seemed pleased, and the talk was positive near the hauler. Scotty had a meeting and left Tim there. "Just stay out of their way."

A few minutes later, his throat parched and the temperature at nearly 90, Tim opened the cooler just outside the hauler and pushed the ice off some soft drinks. He grabbed one and unscrewed the top, then took a hot dog off the grill. Everybody else had already eaten, so Tim figured it would be okay.

As Tim took a bite of the bun, someone with a scratchy voice said, "What do you think you're doing?" Tim turned to see Mac, his grayish brown hair slicked back. He looked like an opossum that had just climbed out of a trash can after a downpour. His face was wrinkled and came to a point in a mouth that looked as sharp as a toothpick. And he held one between his front teeth as he spoke. His eyes were gray and lifeless, like they should belong to one of those mummies in the old movies Tim used to watch late on Saturday nights in Charlie Hale's truck.

"I thought this was for the Maxwell team," Tim said.

Mac snatched the drink, screwed the top on, and jammed it back into the cooler. "It is. And you're not a part of the team. Got it?"

Tim nodded. *I do now.*

Mac took the hot dog and tossed it in the trash. Then he grabbed the remaining three dogs and threw them away too.

Tim just watched, a little amused but still hungry.

Mac disappeared back into the hauler, and Tim felt a hand on his shoulder.

"I see you've met Mac," Dale said.

"Yeah. I didn't know I wasn't supposed to touch any of your food and drinks."

Dale smirked and shook his head, reaching into the cooler and pulling out the drink. "I'll have a talk with Mac. What's ours is yours, okay?"

Tim nodded. "Hey, good time out there. Ninth place isn't bad."

"I'll take it," Dale said. "If I could finish in the top 10, I'll be happy."

"My dad said he was tired of watching drivers just going for points," Tim said. "Said if he was behind the wheel, he'd want to win."

"Your dad was smart," Dale said. "I feel the same way." He turned as someone moved toward them, then looked back at Tim. "I was thinking instead of fighting with Mac about a burger and a hot dog that we'd go back to the hotel and grab something. That okay with you?"

"That'd be fine with me," Tim said. "Breakfast was so good I'd go back there for leftovers."

"Good. We'll be heading into 'happy hour' pretty soon—the last practice session. I want to work out a couple of kinks before I head back."

One of the on-track reporters came up to Dale,

asked how the qualifying had gone, and stuck a mike out.

Dale smiled broadly and didn't miss a beat, mentioning the sponsors up front before answering the question. "I had a good second lap. The first one I got in some loose stuff out there and came up a little short, but I made up for it the second time around. I feel really blessed to have the car working well and a great crew behind me."

"Any predictions for tomorrow?" the reporter said.

"I was just talking with a friend about the whole points versus winning thing, so I'm going to go out there tomorrow and try to get as many points as I can by winning."

"There'll be a few other drivers with something to say about that," the reporter said.

"Ain't that the truth." Dale laughed. "I'll tell you this, racing is just like life—90 percent of it's staying out of trouble and staying on the move, so that's what I'm going to try and do."

Chapter 18
Abraham's Choice

JAMIE FINISHED WORK in time to eat a sandwich, change, and get ready for the Saturday evening service at church. Her mom liked to go on Saturday night when Dad raced on Sunday. Jamie hopped in the Suburban as her mom and Kellen were pulling out. She figured that when you were trying to impress your mother, one of the best places to go was church.

"Got the money for the car today," Jamie said, beaming.

"Really?" her mom said.

Jamie acted as if there were nothing wrong between the two of them. Just ignore the problem and it'll go away—that was her philosophy. And maybe if she played it right, her mom would decide she was ready for the racing school.

"Yep, already deposited it."

"Great," her mom said.

"Not going to spend it on a haircut and nails?" Kellen said.

She would have punched him if she could reach him. Then she was glad she couldn't. She ignored him and smiled, the good girl.

At church Jamie saw Cassie heading up to the nursery and quickly told her what had happened with the man who wrote the bad check.

"See, that's what prayer will do!"

"Yeah, I guess."

"No, seriously, I woke up at about 6:30 this morning and was thinking about you. I asked God to help you be firm and to keep you safe. Did you run into any problems?"

"No," she lied. "The guy was really sorry."

"Now the big question. Have you talked with your mom about the driving school?"

She shook her head, and the music started in the sanctuary. "I'd better go find them. I'll talk with you later."

"I'll be praying," Cassie said.

The Saturday night service was a little more contemporary—meaning the music had an actual beat to it, and there were younger people singing up front. Sometimes the worship team did a drama to illustrate the sermon, and that's what happened this time.

A man who worked at the local radio station and had a voice like a bass drum walked out with a huge walking stick in one hand and cradling something under his other arm. He wore a fake beard; a long, flowing robe; and sandals.

A spotlight hit him, and the rest of the lights went out. He sat and leaned the stick against a fake rock. "Have you ever had something that was hard to give up? something you loved so much that you wanted to hold on to it? you thought there was no way you could ever let it go?"

The congregation was quiet, and the pause of the man made it even quieter.

"I heard from *him* recently. I used to think hearing his voice would be the most wonderful thing. If he would just tell me what to do, I'd do it." He chuckled. "Now I'm not sure I want to hear the voice.

"My wife and I were unable to have children. That was a difficult thing for her, of course, but we rested in the promise that God would give us a child someday." He stood and ran a hand through his hair. "Unfortunately we took matters into our own hands. . . . But then something wonderful happened. She conceived and bore a child, a beautiful son. He's asleep just over there."

The man paced onstage, distraught. "I just don't understand. How could he ask me to do this? I want to have grandchildren and watch my family grow. But if I follow what he's saying to me . . . none of that will come true."

The man continued with his monologue, and Jamie thought it was good but evidently not as good as a lot of the older people in the audience thought it was. Several around her sniffed and cried.

He ended by holding out the bundle in his arms. "This is my son's favorite blanket. His mother made it for him, and it keeps him warm each night. I can't imagine taking it back to his mother empty, but if I follow what God has told me . . ."

He looked at the people in the audience. "Has he spoken to you about laying something down in faith? giving him something dear to you and letting him take control of it? Are you struggling with giving *all* to him?"

He picked up his walking stick and held the blanket close. "I'm not sure about you, but I can't withhold anything from one who has blessed me so much. His plan is much better than the one I have. If I can only do what he asks . . ."

Jamie looked over at her mom, who had her arm around Kellen, hugging him tight.

No one clapped as the man walked into the shadows and the pastor stepped onto the platform. "Maybe you recognize the story of Abraham and Isaac. But I think from your reaction that's not just some story we read in the Bible—it's something that's happening in our lives continually. God has a way of asking us to give him the very thing that's most precious to us. Maybe it's a dream we have. Maybe it's a relationship—a spouse or a close friend. Or in the case of Abraham, it was his child. . . ."

Jamie glanced at her mother again and saw a tear streak down her face. Jamie sat back and listened to the pastor as he shared the whole story of Abraham and how God wanted to do a lot more through him than Abraham could ever imagine.

"Listen to what the angel of the Lord says to Abraham. 'This is what the Lord says: Because you have obeyed me and have not withheld even your son, your only son, I swear by my own name that I will certainly bless you. I will multiply your descendants beyond number, like the stars in the sky and the sand on the seashore. Your descendants will conquer the cities of their enemies. And through your descendants all the nations of the earth will be blessed—all because you have obeyed me.'

"You see, God wants to do something special in your life. And he wants to do it by you voluntarily giving him what is dearest to you. Maybe you've never given your own life, and you're holding on to it because you think God is going to make you do something hard. That he's going to mess with your plans. Well, he may do that—what he gives may be hard, but you'll never truly be fulfilled and satisfied until you let him take over."

The pastor stepped back into the shadows, and the radio guy who was Abraham took his place. This time he stood with his arm around a young, smiling boy. The boy held the blanket in his arms, and the two grinned as they walked down the aisle to the back of the church.

Chapter 19
Elephant

TIM WATCHED COVERAGE on SPEED until Dale got back to the hotel. In all the years he'd traveled with his dad, he'd never eaten in a hotel restaurant or been able to watch the day's coverage in a hotel room.

Dale had gotten hung up with T.J., his crew chief, about some things regarding the race, plus some "things going on with the sponsor." He finally came in and smiled at Tim. "Let's head downstairs. They have a table waiting."

Tim felt like he could eat a horse he was so hungry, and when he looked at the dinner menu in the restaurant, he was surprised they didn't serve grilled horse. They served everything else. He finally picked a cheeseburger, and Dale had some kind of pasta dish. He said it was a good prerace meal that gave him energy.

Tim knew there were racers who had superstitions—they would wear the same old T-shirt under their fire suit or eat the exact same meal as the week or year before when they won a race.

Dale said he didn't have any of those except he always prayed with the chaplain and kissed his wife. "That's not as much of a superstition as it is a priority and a focus. If that's the last time I ever talk to my wife, I want her to know I love her."

"Why do you pray?" Tim said. "You'd be able to talk to him on the other side when you got killed, wouldn't you?"

Dale smiled. "I guess you're right. I think it's more to tell him I know my life is in his hands, and I'm okay with whatever happens."

The waitress came back with their food and a refill for Tim's soda. There were a couple other drivers having late dinners too, and both of them gave a wave or a nod as they passed. Most drivers, like Butch Devalon, were in their big motor coaches or out on the town, Tim guessed. He'd always wondered what it would be like to actually eat and travel with the drivers. They were pretty much gone as soon as the race was over, flying home in their helicopters or airplanes.

When they had finished their meal, the waitress came again and showed them the dessert menu.

Tim eyed the chocolate sundae and then noticed the price.

"You feel like some dessert?" Dale said.

"I'm pretty full."

"That sundae looks good."

"Yeah, if I could pack in any more, I'd order that."

"Why don't you wrap up a sundae to go and he'll eat it in the room," Dale said to the waitress.

"Anything for you, sir?"

Dale slapped his stomach with both hands. "Any more and I'll finish at the back of the pack tomorrow."

The waitress went away, then came back with a bag. She handed the check to Dale and pushed another piece of paper toward him. "My son is a big racing fan. I don't mean to impose, but—"

"Not at all," Dale said. "What's his name?"

She told him. "Oh, he'll be so thrilled."

Dale reached into his pocket and pulled out a small pin with the NASCAR logo on it. "I don't have any hats with me, but give him this and tell him to holler real loud tomorrow."

The woman beamed. "Oh, thank you so much. This is great. I really appreciate it."

When they got back to the room, Tim watched SPEED while Dale made a phone call. From his conversation, Tim guessed he'd called the PR person for the team.

Dale gave the name of the waitress and said, "She's got a son who's a fan. Can you take a hat or a shirt down and give it to her? . . . Yeah, I know we can't give all of it away, but I think it'll mean something to her. . . . Great. Thanks."

Dale sat at a round table in the corner and took off his boots, looking out at the golf course.

It seemed like there was something on Dale's mind, but Tim figured if he wanted to talk, he'd say so.

"If you don't mind, Tim, why don't you turn that off and come over here and have a seat."

Tim did and opened the bag with the sundae in a Styrofoam container. The ride up the elevator had made just enough room for dessert. And the ice cream was the right consistency—soft and gooey and mixing well with the chocolate and caramel.

"Did you ever get the letter I sent to you?" Dale said.

"No, I don't believe I did. What did it say?"

Dale pursed his lips. "Well, I kind of explained some things. Tell me this. You ever heard of the elephant in the room?"

"No, sir."

"Do you know what it means?"

"Does it have anything to do with the circus?"

Dale tried to hide his smile. "No. It means there's something that needs to be talked about, but everybody is avoiding the touchy topic. And the more you *don't* talk about it, the bigger the thing gets."

Tim ate a big spoonful of ice cream and chocolate so he wouldn't have to say anything.

Dale leaned forward and put his hat on the table and folded his hands. "I want to talk about Talladega last year."

Tim closed his eyes. The sights and sounds of the track came back to him. The reaction of the crowd when the accident happened. The sirens. The lady he thought might be his mother but wasn't. The security guys looking for him. The helicopter flying away.

"Okay," Tim said. "That was the worst day of my life."

"Mine too. To know that I was involved in the accident that caused your dad's death was something hard for me to live with. Part of me didn't want to ever get on the track again."

"What do you mean, 'involved'?" Tim said. "You weren't just involved—you were the one who caused it."

Dale talked about the race—the conditions at the track, the weather, the mood of the drivers. "A few laps before the accident, the #53 car started spurting some brake fluid. One of his lines was cut. As he was going to the pits, he dropped a lot of that on the front end of pit road, right where my stall was. So that area was slick to start off."

"So it was slick," Tim said. "That still doesn't excuse you for coming in there as fast as you did."

Dale sighed. "There's no video of the accident. As many camera angles as they have, they didn't catch this one. But I can assure you, Tim, that I never meant to hurt your dad. And I'd do anything if I could bring him back."

"That's why you're offering me a place to stay. You feel guilty about it and want to try and make it up to me."

"I can never make up for your dad. It's not possible. But my wife and I have talked about adopting a baby from another country, giving some child a chance to grow up here. We can't have any more children, and it's something we both feel we want to do. When the accident happened, Nicole and I both had a feeling that this was our chance. And when I contacted your social worker and told her about our idea, she let me know you might like a change."

Suddenly Tim didn't feel like eating anymore. He put down his spoon and closed the Styrofoam lid. "So you felt sorry for me. I'm okay with that."

"I've never met you before last night. I did know

your dad a little from the chapel services, and I talked with Charlie Hale about you."

Tim blushed. "Don't believe everything he says about me."

"I don't want you to feel like we pity you. We want to give you a good home for as long as you need it, some encouragement along the way, and a shot at life. That's what I wanted to say."

"I appreciate it," Tim said. "I was wondering when we'd get around to that elephant. But something's bothering me."

"Go ahead."

"Sounds to me like you're saying something happened on the track that led to the accident. I haven't heard that before. I read the report about it in one of the magazines. It was just a blurb."

Dale nodded. "I can't go into it in detail, but I was pushed. I lost control, and the tires skidded on that wet surface."

"Then who—?"

Dale held up a hand. "I'm sure you want to know more, but let's just leave it here."

Tim got up and opened the refrigerator in the kitchenette. He tossed in what was left of the sundae, closed the door, and headed to the front door.

"Tim?"

"I'm going down to the pool and have a look around," Tim said, not turning around.

"That's fine. Just one more thing."

"Yeah?"

"I think your dad would be proud of the way you've handled everything. Real proud."

Tim still didn't turn around. He just said, "Yeah" and walked into the hallway.

Chapter 20
Sunday Morning Coming Down

THE RIDE HOME was quiet for Jamie and her mom. Kellen couldn't quit talking about his friend Paul, who had played Isaac in the service. "Didn't have anything to say, but he did a good job."

"It was a powerful drama," Jamie's mom said. "What did you think, Jamie?"

"Yeah, it was good."

Jamie went to her room and stayed there the rest of the night. The phone rang late, and she saw it was her dad's cell phone, but she didn't pick up. She wondered if the guy from Florida had made it and how things had gone, but there was too much on her mind. Too many things spinning around.

She tossed and turned through the night and dreamed she was at a track—it was the Texas Motor Speedway—standing near pit road. A dark figure lurked behind the wall, and Jamie moved toward the end of pit road. But as she neared the spot where the ambulance was parked and the emergency medical personnel milled about, the dark figure darted toward her. Scared, she ran around the ambulance, trying to get away. Her feet hit grass, but in front of her was a chain-link fence.

Jamie vaulted the fence and ran toward the apron of the track, followed closely by the figure. A thunderous sound approached, and she looked back, seeing a line of cars, three deep, heading straight for her. She ran faster, but her feet were like lead. She fell and covered her head, sure that she would be flattened by the cars.

She looked back quickly and saw her father's face through the windshield. That face comforted her for a moment but then turned into Butch Devalon's, his dark sunglasses glinting in the sunlight. He swerved right toward Jamie.

She awakened, pulled the cover from over her head, and noticed the sun peeking over the trees. She sat up and stretched, yawning, and quickly dressed in her sweats. She stole downstairs, smelling coffee brewing, and saw her mother at the kitchen table. She had her Bible open and the phone to her ear.

Jamie slipped outside to her car and drove to the fitness center. Other drivers had their own gyms in their homes or at the nearby garage, and she'd bugged her dad about putting one in, but it was no use.

She threw herself into the workout, alternating between weights and the bike or treadmill. She had a section on her audio player with songs just the right length for each station in the workout. The TVs overhead were tuned to the Sunday morning news shows. There were heads talking—a guy in a military uniform, a woman senator—and one had the vice president. He didn't look too happy with the interviewer.

TVs over the treadmills were tuned to SPEED and gave updates on the race in Texas. They replayed highlights of yesterday's race and the qualifier for this afternoon.

All through the exercise and music and TV images, Jamie couldn't shake the feeling from last night. It wasn't the dream that stuck with her but what the pastor had said and the look on her mother's face. The more she thought about it, the more she pumped the weights, and the more convinced she was that her mother's tears had been for her. Jamie was sure her mother was crying because she thought Jamie needed to give her dreams and her life to God. She closed her eyes as she bench-pressed the weights.

Chapter 21
Chapel

"NICOLE AND I HAVE decided we're not going to force you to go to church services," Dale said to Tim as they walked toward the media center. They'd bought several shirts, a jacket, and a hat at the concession area, and Tim had stuck them in his suitcase in the hauler.

"Of course, we hope you'll want to go with us, but we're not going to make you," Dale said.

"Okay," Tim said.

"There's a chapel service right after the drivers' meeting, so you can stay or head back to the hauler if you'd like."

Tim looked around and spotted who he thought was the chaplain—an older guy with a bad suit. He didn't want to go, but he figured it wasn't a good idea to annoy Dale just before the race. Sure, Tim was ticked that Dale wouldn't tell him who had pushed him at Talladega, but he assumed Dale had a good reason for not saying anything yet.

"I'll stay," Tim said.

Tim tried not to stare at the famous drivers sitting around him, but it was kind of hard. Faces he saw plastered all over magazines and TV commercials were just a few seats from him. He'd never seen so many sunglasses in one place in all his life. There were also officials scattered around the room and family members of the drivers and the crew chiefs.

The drivers were laughing and joking until the leader stood up. He had a voice like a bullhorn, so he didn't really need the microphone, but he used it anyway. He talked about the rules of the race, some of the different aspects of the track, and the speed to maintain on pit road. He asked if there were any questions, and everybody just looked at one another.

"All right, let's stand as the chaplain comes to lead us in prayer. And right afterward, for those who want to stay, there's going to be a short service."

To Tim's surprise, the guy with the bad suit stayed at his seat, and a younger guy who looked like he worked out twice a day went to the front. He had curly hair and wore a nice pair of jeans. He smiled and said, "Let's pray."

Tim looked around and saw everybody had taken off their hats, so he grabbed his. A lot of the guys kept their eyes open, but he glanced at Dale, and his eyes were shut tight.

When the prayer was over, almost everybody said, "Amen," especially the wives of the drivers.

Dale sat back down, but the rest of the room looked like a sale at Target on the day after Thanksgiving. Or like the plug had been pulled on the bathtub, and the drivers were the water heading for the drain.

When the room cleared, the chaplain welcomed newcomers and checked his watch. "We have only 12 minutes today, so let me get right to the point. We've been going through the book of James. . . ."

Tim mentally checked out and focused on the sounds surrounding the building. The jet blowers cleaned debris from the track and nearly drowned out the chaplain. Radios crackled as security people passed. Cars revved. Tim's stomach fluttered in anticipation of the race, and he couldn't believe that someone just about to go to battle on the track would sit as calm as Dale and listen intently to a guy a lot younger read from the Bible, but here they were.

". . . which takes us back to verses three and four of the first chapter: 'For you know that when your faith is tested, your endurance has a chance to grow. So let it grow, for when your endurance is fully developed, you will be perfect and complete, needing nothing.'

"You see, a lot of people think life is supposed to be perfect—no problems, no difficulties, all tidy and nice like a hotel room that's just been cleaned. But life is messy and we make mistakes, and God's way of perfecting us is to walk through the grime with us."

Tim watched the people bow their heads around him. He looked up at the chaplain, and the guy was looking straight back at him.

The chaplain smiled and then closed his eyes and prayed.

Chapter 22
Couch Talk

"CAN I TALK WITH YOU a minute?" Jamie's mom said when Jamie came in the front door.

"I'm kind of grubby—I was going to take a shower and come down before the race starts." The house was unusually quiet. "Where's Kellen?"

"He went to Sunday school. Then over to Paul's house."

Little show-off, Jamie thought.

Her mom patted the couch and said, "Come over and sit a minute. I don't care if you're grubby."

She had the TV in the living room turned down and a cup of coffee in her hand. The pits were swarming with people in colorful uniforms, and reports about racers had begun.

"I saw Dad qualified in the ninth position," Jamie said. "That's a lot better."

"He was really happy about it when I talked with him this morning. He said to say hi."

Jamie stared at the TV. "Aren't the people from your Bible study coming over?"

Her mom shook her head. "I told them we wanted to be alone this weekend. They'll still be praying—"

"Look! There's Dad's car!" Jamie interrupted. She grabbed the remote and turned up the volume.

The reporter was standing in front of the Maxwell crash cart talking about a conversation he'd had yesterday. "And you could tell how excited Dale was to finally crack the top 10 in the hunt for the pole."

Her dad's face was covered with sweat, his hair matted. He was smiling as broadly as she could ever remember. "I had a good second lap. The first one I got in some loose stuff out there. . . ."

"Who's that?" Jamie said, looking at a dark-haired guy almost hiding behind her dad.

"That must be Tim," her mom said. "He flew to Dallas and is at the race. They'll come home this evening."

Jamie stared at her. "That was my idea." She closed her eyes, realizing how angry that sounded, then tried to recover. "Are you putting him in the guest room?"

"That's what I'd planned. I've put some things in there I'm hoping will make him feel at home."

Her dad's face disappeared, and the camera focused on the building at the far end of the infield as the reporter began again. "You can bet Dale and a few others are inside this tent right now. This is where the prerace chapel is held—you can see some of them heading toward the track now. As you probably know, Dale is a religious guy and attends this meeting each week. We'll see if his connections upstairs bring him any better luck. Back to you, guys."

"Well, being religious hasn't helped much in the last year," a commentator said.

Jamie's mom turned down the sound and put her coffee mug on the table. "There's something we need to talk about. I've been thinking a lot about—"

Jamie scooted forward and shook her head. "You don't have to say anything more, Mom. I know what you're thinking, and I've made my own decision."

Her mother's eyebrows came together in a tight squeeze. "How could you know what I'm thinking?"

Jamie sighed. "I know how you feel about me and . . . God. And when that pastor talked about letting go of what's dearest to us, I knew you thought about me and how I should give up racing. That it's becoming the biggest thing in my life—"

"You have no idea what I'm thinking," her mom said.

"I know you want me to be a better Christian and be more like Cassie. I see the way you look at her when she sings up front or works in the nursery."

"Jamie, I can't believe you'd say that!"

"So I've made my decision. I'm going to give up racing and be a nun or something."

Her mom turned her head, and at first Jamie thought she'd made her cry. Instead, when her mom turned back she was laughing, her shoulders shaking.

"What did I say?"

"The first NASCAR nun," her mom choked. "That's the funniest thing I've ever heard."

Jamie tried not to smile, but she couldn't help it. "Seriously, Mom, you don't want me to move ahead—you want me to stay your little girl and be safe. I'm probably not good enough to go further anyway."

Her mother stopped smiling, and Jamie stared at the screen.

"Jamie, look at me."

When Jamie wouldn't, her mom turned the TV off.

"You're going to miss the start," Jamie said.

"Look at me."

Jamie did.

"It's true that I want you to have a relationship with God. I've prayed for that for years. But I don't want you to be Cassie Strower or any of the other kids at that church. I want you to be Jamie Maxwell. I want you to be who God created you to be."

Jamie looked at the blank screen, but she could see her mother's face in the reflection.

"Now I want you to listen to something," her mother continued. "You want to know what touched me the most during that sermon last night? It wasn't the thought of you giving up racing—it was the thought of me giving up you."

Jamie turned. "I don't get it."

"Abraham could have held on to his son and not let him out of his sight. He was the dearest thing in the world to him. But instead, he trusted what God said and followed his leading. He gave his son back to God and allowed him to take control." Jamie's mom stared at the couch, as if she were searching for an earring she'd dropped. "And that's what I've decided to do with you."

"What do you mean?" Jamie said.

"I've known you've had these dreams. I've known what direction you were going. And I've tried to encourage you along the way. But last night I saw clearly that God has made you interested in racing for a reason, and though it's not my plan, I don't want my plan. I want his. I want to see what he's going to do with you. Just the fact that you thought about the message this long means God is working on your heart."

Jamie didn't speak, afraid her mom might change her mind if she did.

"It's kind of like being on a crew and standing by the wall, waiting for your chance. At some point, you have to jump in and get to work. And that's what I'm doing. Going over the wall with you."

"Have you talked with Dad about this?" Jamie finally said.

She nodded.

"So what does that mean? That I can go to the school?"

Her mom grabbed the Yellow Pages from under the phone. "Yeah, but we'll need to get something before that."

"What are you looking for?"

"Do you know where they sell nun's outfits?"

Jamie laughed out loud. Her mother moved closer and hugged her, and Jamie hugged her back. Just a little. As they embraced, Jamie spoke softly. "That part about Cassie. Isn't it true that you'd like to see me be interested in missionaries and memorizing verses and serving God and all that?"

Jamie's mom pulled back and locked eyes with her. "I've prayed every day that you would know and experience God's love. That you'd follow him. But that's not something I can force on you, and I know if I try, it could actually push you away from him. That's a decision you're going to have to make."

"I'm scared that if I really give my racing to God, he'll take it away from me."

"I used to think that way too. That when we came to God, he wanted to punish us for the bad things we'd done. Or that he wanted to hide what was good from us. But you know what I think now? I believe God wires each one of us differently and gives us unique dreams and desires. Until we find that passion and follow it, we just kind of wander around trying to feel better about feeling so bad.

"Maybe your passion and purpose is racing, and you'll be able to do that and praise God with your driving. Or when you reach my age, your desire might change."

Jamie listened and thought of the pastor's words. She'd thought her mom had been thinking of her through the whole sermon, but she'd been thinking about herself. "What's *your* passion and purpose?"

"Right now it's to give as much as I can to you and your brother, to love my husband well, and to be there for Tim. Now when you kids are grown and gone, I might become an astronaut or a pro wrestler. . . ."

"Or adopt a baby from Zimbabwe."

Jamie's mom smiled. "Here's what I know: the best thing you can do with your life is give your heart to God and let him take control. His plan is so much better than anything we can come up with. But that took me a long time to figure out. I want to keep you from pain and wrong decisions, but you're getting old enough to make those decisions yourself."

"So I can go to the driving school?"

"You've worked really hard to get here, Jamie, and I'm proud of you. I not only want you to go to that school—I want you to come out number one. You understand?"

"Number one in a nun's habit," Jamie said.

Chapter 23
Texas Motor Speedway

TIM STOOD BEHIND the pit box and watched the crew pace and try to relax. T.J. was out by the car with Dale, talking and gesturing. When he returned, he gave Tim a set of headphones and a radio. "Dale said he wanted you to be able to hear our chatter. You want to come up top with us?"

Tim shook his head and thanked him for the headphones. The pit box was the place to be during a race, but truth be told, Tim didn't like heights very much and the box was high. Sure, it had the umbrellas that shielded you from the sun and the computer screens that had all the race info, but just one look down was enough to keep Tim away.

The crew wore their fire suits and gloves and had their shoes laced tightly, checking everything two or three times.

Cal, the jackman, stretched by putting one leg on a stack of tires and leaning forward. He was in a zone, focusing on the task ahead. He might not even touch the car for the first 40 laps, but then the whole process would boil down to 12 to 15 seconds—if everybody got through their jobs clean.

Mac walked up, pulling a cart with two gas cans behind him, stopping and scowling at Tim as he tried to get to the wall. Tim wasn't really in the way—at least he didn't think he was—but Mac made him pay. He pointed to the ground and a yellow line that was painted on the concrete. Mac pulled one earphone away from Tim's ear. "Stay behind that line. You block me when I'm coming toward the car, and I'll have you kicked out of here."

Tim nodded. "Yes, sir."

Mac grabbed the cart and started toward the wall. He turned and scowled again as the two grand marshals—a former football player and a guy from a popular TV show—yelled, "Gentlemen, start your engines!"

"I'm not trying to be mean," Mac shouted over the thunderous noise. "You don't want to mess up our pit stops. That's why I'm telling you to stay back. Understand?"

"Sure do," Tim said. "I used to go to tracks with my dad."

Mac stared at him. “I knew your daddy. He was a good man. Now stay back, you hear?”

Tim nodded and looked at his watch. It was 1:22 when the pace car took off and led the cars in the first trip around the track. When the green flag flew, the crowd of more than 200,000 rose and cheered, and Tim could almost hear them over the roar of the engines.

He focused on Dale through the window net and pumped a fist in the air and yelled. Rather than resenting Dale and holding him responsible for his dad’s death, Tim had been won over. He wondered what it would be like to join his family, but he figured if they were half as nice as Dale, things would be okay.

Tim looked back at the leader pole and saw Dale had slipped to the #13 position after only five laps. Then he heard Scotty’s voice on the radio.

“Got a spinout behind you in turn four, Dale,” Scotty said. “Yellow flag.”

The car that had trouble didn’t have enough damage to pit, so the race resumed in four laps. Dale had fought his way up to 10th when the second yellow came out at lap 25. This time the #55 car slammed the wall entering turn three and had to take his car behind the wall.

“Well, looks like we can’t do any worse than 42nd place.” Dale chuckled.

"Gonna be a lot higher than that today, Dale," T.J. said. "You look good out there. Car looks smooth in the turns."

"Yeah, if I can get out of some of this traffic here, I should be good."

"Looks like you're pitting in another lap," T.J. said. "What do you need?"

Tim glanced at the crew and noticed that as soon as the caution came out, everyone was right in position at the wall.

Dale said, "Getting a little push on the right side. Maybe just change the two right and a splash."

The crew made a flurry of hand signals as Dale and the other drivers rumbled into the pits. Dale's spot was close to the front of pit road, and Tim craned his neck to see him. Before Dale had even stopped inside the box, Cal had the jack out. He looked like he was flying through the air as he slid it under the car and pumped twice to lift it. The air wrenches gave short bursts up and down the line.

Tim thought he heard something and looked at the crowd. People were standing, some pointing.

"One one thousand, two one thousand," Tim counted.

"Got a jam behind you," Scotty said. "Get out of there fast!"

Ten cars back, the lead racer had made contact

with another car coming down pit road. Their cars collided, creating a chain reaction behind them.

"Let's go! Let's go!" Dale yelled.

". . . eight one thousand, nine one thousand . . ."

The crew finished, and Dale pulled out in front of the cars behind him. "Good job back there, guys."

Chapter 24
The Feed

JAMIE HOPPED ONTO THE COUCH with wet hair just as the race began.

They heard Scotty's and her dad's voices from the satellite feed as well as the special in-car camera feed in the upper right-hand corner of the screen. It cost more, but her dad had decided it was worth it for the family to be able to watch the races from his perspective anytime they wanted. The rest of the screen was the network feed of the race.

When the grand marshals said the famous words, "Gentlemen, start your engines!" her dad put his right hand up in an L and then pointed to the camera.

Her mom mimicked the move and whispered, "I love you too, sweetie."

"This is almost enough to make me sick," Jamie said, laughing.

Jamie and her mom watched the

race unfold, listening to the communication between driver and crew members. Jamie screamed at every opening, urging her dad to take them, sometimes jumping up to the TV and pointing at spots where she thought he could pass.

When a caution sent them to pit road, Jamie clapped. "Now! Come on, just take right side tires! Get back on the track!"

Her dad picked up four spots from a quick pit stop and was sixth when the green flag came out again.

"This is great!" Jamie squealed.

"It's a long race, but he seems to be doing better." Her mom moved closer to the TV each time the pit area was shown, and Jamie guessed she was looking for Tim.

Another caution came out on lap 77 for debris on the track. The leaders made their second pit stop of the day, and it was a race back to the track. Watching the crews jump out on the cars was nerve-racking for Jamie. She knew how many races were won or lost simply because a lug nut wouldn't go on or come off.

"Come on! Come on!" she said, pacing.

"He's coming out," her mom said.

The #37 car, in the lead before the pit stop, hit the exit just before her dad.

The announcer said, ". . . and what a great pit stop

for Dale Maxwell in the #14 car, moving into second place now."

The camera showed the Maxwell crew clapping and slapping high fives.

"I owe you guys one," her dad said on the radio.

"Great job, everyone," Scotty said.

The announcer made a comment about some adjustments to the #37 car, and Jamie got excited again. "I know what Dad has to do," she said. "Since #37 is real tight, he's vulnerable low. Dad has to go into the turn high and drop down and he'll have the lead."

In the 99th lap, that's exactly what happened. In turn one, #14 went high, dropped to the bottom, and shot underneath #37 into the straightaway for the lead.

Shots of the crowd waving and cheering flashed onscreen, but Jamie and her mom barely noticed because they were screaming and hugging each other.

Two laps later, another car spun out and flew across the grass on the infield.

The yellow flag came out, and Jamie's dad said, "Just in time. I need four new tires, guys. I'm not giving up this lead, so let's make this a good one."

The onscreen clock counted up as Cal jumped on the right side of the car and the tires came off.

Jamie watched, her mouth agape, in awe of the way the team worked. She'd had a crush on Cal since she was 14 but not because he was so attractive—which he was. He was also the nicest guy on the team, and he helped out with some of the midweek youth activities at the church.

Jamie's hands perspired, and she rubbed them against her shorts and bit her lower lip.

Her mother kept a hand over her mouth, staring at the upper right-hand corner of the screen as Jamie's dad got a quick drink of Gatorade and tossed the bottle out the window.

"Dale Maxwell comes out of the pits first," the announcer said. "The pit crew got him out of there in 14.2—not too shabby."

"Yeah, they're really firing on all cylinders now," the commentator said. "And Dale sure looks like he's driving with new life. Maybe he got something extra in that chapel service today, huh? Maybe a little extra power?"

"We'll see if he can hold this slim lead. . . ."

Chapter 25
Chasing the Leader

TIM WALKED DOWN PIT ROAD, careful not to get in anybody's way. Several cars had already been taken to the garage, and their pit boxes had been removed. One driver who was involved in a nasty crash had been taken to the infield care center, and Tim watched as the man's wife, sparkling with lots of jewelry (even her sunglasses had diamonds), was escorted to the center.

The sun baked him, but he wouldn't have wanted to be anywhere else. The sounds and sights sent a surge of excitement through him, and he felt like this was what he wanted to do—to race like Dale Maxwell, just like his dad had wanted to do.

The race continued without another yellow flag until lap 304. Dale was in third place when he entered the pits.

With four new tires and a full tank, he roared back to the track in a jam of cars.

Tim switched to the race coverage on the radio. The guys in the booth were saying this might be the last pit stop. "And it looks like Dale Maxwell just took control of this race, boys. He's driving like the old Dale."

As Tim switched the radio back, he wondered what that meant. What was different with Dale now? Cars followed the pace car until it finally trailed off. Tim rubbed his hands together as the green flag flew and the engines roared past the starting line.

"This one is ours, guys," Dale said.

They had gone 324 laps around the 1.5 mile track, only 14 miles from the finish of the 500-mile race, when a black car, #13, blew through the pack and into second position behind Dale.

"Oh no," Tim muttered.

"Stay low. Stay low," Scotty said. "You got Devalon coming up high. He's swapping paint with just about everybody behind you."

The radio clicked twice.

"Right behind him is #27."

The radio clicked again.

Tim knew that #27 was Butch Devalon's teammate. They would try to push Dale and overtake him if they could.

"Come on," Tim mumbled.

"You got 'em, Dale," T.J. said. "Just stay in the groove."

Tim remembered the first year #27 raced for the cup. His father had said the guy didn't deserve to race at the top level. "Last year he hit everything on the track but the lottery." The memory made Tim smile.

Dale stayed low around the track with the two Devalon cars right behind him. When the white flag came out, signaling the last lap, #13 and #27 were side by side, following Dale by less than a car length.

"One more, Dale," T.J. said. "You can do it."

Dale came up on a slower car in the middle of the track just before the first turn.

"Stay low. Stay low," Scotty said. "Coming up on the right is #13. At your bumper."

They hit the turn, and Tim watched Dale sail around the corner and into the backstretch. He lost him in the line of haulers and RVs, so he instinctively looked at the stands and all the eyes riveted on the three cars. He looked at the computer screen, but crew members were bunched up in front of it. He moved to the wall as the lead cars screamed into turns three and four. Tim glanced at the starter, who grabbed the checkered flag and held it like it was a life vest in a hurricane.

"Go high," Scotty said. "Stay high. Stay high. . . ."

A plume of smoke rose from the back turn.

Chapter 26
Thrilling End

JAMIE AND HER MOM held on to each other in front of the TV. The announcers' voices rose as the racers neared the end of the 500th mile. Jamie could hardly watch, but there was no way she was *not* going to watch.

"The big question is, can Dale Maxwell pull it out?" the commentator said. "Can he beat a faster Devalon team breathing down his neck?"

"They're in turn three, Butch Devalon coming hard—Oh!—"

"He clipped him!"

"Can you believe that?"

"No!" Jamie screamed at the TV.

"He's into the wall hard on that one," the commentator said. "It looked like Butch was going to try and slingshot out of there, and when Dale moved down to block, he got into the #27 car. That's a shame."

"Butch Devalon avoids the crash and takes the checkered flag in a thrilling end to this race at the Texas Speedway."

Jamie and her mom fell onto the couch together, the air coming out of the entire room. "I can't believe he did that."

The replay showed that as Dale moved down, Devalon had nudged his teammate into Maxwell. There was discussion about whether it was on purpose.

"And here are the official results. . . ."

Jamie's heart fell. Her dad had gone from winning the race to finishing 23rd. The looks on the faces of the pit crew said it all. Cal slammed his gloves onto the pavement. T.J. leaned back in his chair and shook his head. Worst of all, the in-car camera had gone out at the crash impact.

The TV coverage was ending, and Butch Devalon was doing his little victory dance that looked to Jamie like a duck trying to get out of a cold pond. Just before they cut away, the camera focused on the #14 car and the driver, not moving inside the car.

Chapter 27
Finger-Pointing

TIM STOOD at the infield care center door, watching the Devalon car being pushed to the garage. NASCAR would take the engine apart piece by piece and inspect it to make sure there was nothing funny about it.

A few yards away, a camera crew encircled Butch Devalon, and Tim could hear him babbling on. "It was a great race, and I hate like the dickens to see Dale taken out of it like that when he'd been leading for so long," he said. "I take my hat off to him. He took a big chance staying out there, and it almost paid off for him."

"What happened at the end?" a reporter said, shoving the microphone back at Devalon.

"I got a little antsy there trying to get past him. What I wanted to do was go way low and let my teammate go high and see if either of us could get a clear shot at the finish, but we kind of bunched up. It was just one of those racing things."

The reporter asked another question, but Devalon held up a hand and looked straight into the camera. "Before I go on, I want to dedicate this race to my son, Chad. A lot of you know he got into a wreck on a track back home this past week, and he was pretty banged up. So this one's for you, Chad. Woo-hoo!"

"How does it feel to be leading the points race at this stage of the season?" another reporter said.

"Oh, we got a long way to go, but I'd rather be leading than chasing anytime—that's for sure."

Tim turned away and walked around the building. On the other side was a concessions stand, and the people were packing up and locking coolers. His stomach growled and ached. He'd been so focused on the race that he hadn't eaten anything.

A commotion behind him made him turn to see Dale walking out of the back of the building and into a gauntlet of reporters. He had a white bandage around his left hand and walked a little slowly, but he looked okay to Tim. T.J. was there waiting and spoke with Dale.

The reporters shouted questions at Dale until they surrounded him and made him stop moving, but he still craned his neck above the cameras and microphones, looking for something. Or someone. When he saw Tim, he waved and gave him a thumbs-up. He turned to T.J. and said something.

The crew chief got out of the pack and came over to Tim. "Dale wants you to stay right here until he's done with these people, okay?"

"Yes, sir. Is he okay?"

"I think he's all right, but I've never seen him this mad before."

"You weren't moving out there, Dale," a reporter asked. "What happened?"

"Well, you hit the wall as hard as I did and you'll find out. I guess the reason I didn't move was a mixture of shock and disbelief about what had happened. And there wasn't a whole lot I could do but just sit there and watch the guys pass me."

"Talk about that final turn, Dale. Did you think you had the finish line?"

"Yeah, I knew we had a good car today, and I just wanted to punch it out of that fourth turn there, but it didn't work out like I wanted."

"Devalon said it was one of those racing things. Do you agree with that?"

Dale pushed his hat back a little and scratched at his hair. "Yeah. I suppose it was."

"What do you want to say to Devalon?" another reporter said.

"I don't know that *saying* something is what I would do right now. And if I did, I'd probably have to ask forgiveness for it later." Dale smiled. "Thank you, guys. I need to get back to my team. They did a great job out there today, but I couldn't finish it the way I wanted. Excuse me." He pushed his way through the crowd and waved at Tim to catch up with him.

Soon the media members left, and it was just Tim, Dale, and T.J.

"You okay?" Tim said.

"Yeah, I just need to get to a phone and call my wife."

"Here you go," T.J. said, handing Dale a cell phone.

Dale dialed as he walked, passing other crews and drivers who tried to encourage him.

"Tough luck out there today, Dale."

"Nice race, Maxwell."

"You'll get him next week, Dale."

He waved and tried to smile, but Tim could tell he'd been wounded and not just on his body.

"Honey, it's me. . . . No, I'm all right. Jammed my left wrist a little when I hit the wall. . . . Yeah, it was disappointing to say the least. . . . No, I haven't seen him or talked to him, and I can't say that I want to. . . . He's right here with me. We'll head to the airport and be back there early this evening. . . ."

Out of the corner of his eye, Tim saw someone in a black fire suit heading toward them. He came up behind Dale as a lone camera guy followed.

Dale turned. The look on his face when he saw Butch Devalon was priceless, if you're willing to pay for a look that makes dogs cower and little children run away. "Hang on a minute, honey," Dale said, putting the phone away.

"Dale, I want you to know—"

"No," Dale interrupted, pointing a finger at him.

The red light on the camera glowed, and several people came out of a nearby hauler to watch.

T.J. touched Dale's shoulder, but Dale shook him off. "Everything you needed to let me know you showed me on the track. I'm done with it, Butch." Dale clenched his teeth, and it looked like he wanted to say something else, but he turned and walked away.

"Dale, don't act this way," Devalon called after him. "That could just as easily have been me in the wall out there."

Dale stopped, but T.J. put a hand on his back and pushed him forward. "Keep walking. Cameras are rolling. Let's get out of here."

Chapter 28
New Room

TIM COULD TELL that Dale was stiff as he tried to get comfortable in the airplane seat. They didn't talk much on the way home, though Tim did find out how many backup cars they had in the garage and that it wouldn't be a problem to be ready for Phoenix next weekend because that was a one-mile track, and they were going to use a different car anyway.

"Did you want to punch Devalon when he came up to you?" Tim said.

Dale got a far-off look on his face. "Tim, I try to live my life like Jesus did, but I tell you what, I felt like turning old Devalon's tables over on him and getting out my whip."

Tim didn't know whether to laugh or not. "I don't understand."

Dale told him some story about Jesus getting mad at people who were selling stuff in a church. Although Tim didn't follow the whole thing, it made sense. Jesus got mad at people and he was perfect, so getting mad was not the problem. Hauling off and punching somebody or yelling bad words at them was.

/////

The Charlotte airport was a lot like the other airports Tim had been in over the past few days. They got their luggage and took it to the car. Dale drove north, first on the Billy Graham Parkway, then on a couple of other roads.

"Velocity is not all that big," Dale explained, "but it's a nice place to raise a family."

Dale told Tim about Kellen and how much he looked forward to having Tim live with them. He said Jamie was going through a phase and planned on attending a driving school soon. "I wouldn't expect too much from her the first couple days."

"Are you saying she's going to be mean?" Tim said.

"*Mean* isn't the word. Just kind of moody at times. I think growing up is hard for all of us, and her mother and I are trying to help her do that. What I'm saying is, if you find it hard to connect with her, as my wife likes to say, it's not your fault."

/////

Mrs. Maxwell was waiting outside under the porch light when they arrived home. She was a pretty woman with long red hair. She had a thin build and a nice smile. She hugged her husband, not too hard, and shook Tim's hand. "I'm glad to finally get to meet you, Tim. Did you enjoy the race?"

"It was a whole lot of fun until the end," Tim said.

"My feelings exactly," Dale said.

The screen door swung open, and a kid in pajamas came running outside carrying two baseball gloves. "Is this him?"

"Tim, this is Kellen," Dale said.

"Mom said I have to go to bed soon because I have school tomorrow, but we could probably get in a few minutes of catch," Kellen said in one long breath.

"Kellen, Tim has had a long day," Mrs. Maxwell said.

"I'd like to throw a little," Tim said, "but it's kind of dark. How about tomorrow?"

"Good idea," Dale said. "Why don't you take Tim and show him his room?"

"Okay," Kellen said.

Dale hugged his son, and the boy kind of rolled his eyes. "You make it out of the race okay?"

"Yeah, I'll be as good as new in a few days. Show Tim downstairs now."

Tim noticed some shoes in a pile by the door, but he didn't think anything about it. Kellen threw the gloves on the upstairs landing and tossed the ball from hand to hand as they walked downstairs. There were pictures of the family on the wall, and the girl, Jamie, looked more like a model than a race car driver.

The house was clean and had lots of wood floors. The downstairs had thick carpet, and there was an area in the family room with a pool table and a big TV.

"We come down here to watch movies and stuff," Kellen said. "And there's a Ping-Pong table you can throw on top of the pool table."

"That's cool," Tim said, though it didn't even come close to what he was thinking. After living so long with his dad on the road and then in Tyson's trailer, this place was like a castle complete with a moat and a playground.

"This is your room," Kellen said, flipping on the light. "Mom fixed it up for you."

Tim put his suitcase down, and his gaze swept the room. The bed looked so comfortable he wanted to jump in and go to sleep that second. On the walls were pictures of racetracks, drivers, and cars. The closet was bigger than his room back in Florida. He looked down and realized he still had his shoes on and remembered the pile of them upstairs by the door. He'd never been in a house where you actually took off your shoes when you came inside.

Something caught his eye on the nightstand, and he walked over and picked up a picture. It was a photo of his dad he'd never seen before. He was standing behind a couple of racing legends, looking at the camera and smiling.

"The racing chaplain who goes to our church found that for you," Mrs. Maxwell said, stepping into the room. "I thought you'd like it. But if there's anything here you don't like, just tell me and I'll have it taken down."

"It's awesome," Tim said. "The whole thing is . . . like a hotel. Like I'm walking into a dream."

She smiled. "I'm glad you like it."

A girl appeared in the doorway and peeked around Mrs. Maxwell. "Hi, I'm Jamie," she said, smiling. Same smile as her mother. She reached out a hand, and Tim shook. Firm handshake. Kind of rough hands, like she knew how to use tools.

"I-I saw you on the Daytona coverage," Tim said.

"Yeah, I guess a lot of people did," Jamie said. "You need a ride to school?"

"We need to get him situated before he starts," Mrs. Maxwell said.

"Well, if you need a ride, let me know." Jamie turned and started out. It looked like she wanted to say something to her mom, but she didn't.

"Thanks for letting me come here, Mrs. Maxwell," Tim said. He didn't feel right calling her Nicole, though it felt fine calling Mr. Maxwell Dale. "If I do something wrong, let me know. I've never lived in a nice place like this."

Chapter 29
Butch's Offer

JAMIE WALKED INTO the Devalon garage and felt an odd feeling in the pit of her stomach. After what had happened at the Texas race, she felt like coming here was somehow betraying her dad, but she marched to the Devalon office anyway and saw the Texas trophy sitting near the front.

The garage had a light feeling to it—mechanics were laughing and telling jokes and slapping each other's backs. It had been a good year for the team, and already some people were saying there wouldn't need to be a race for the Chase—Butch Devalon was going to win the thing way before Homestead.

Jamie stopped at the office where the woman with the pasted-on smile sat. She looked a little more naturally cheerful this time. When Jamie asked if Mr. Devalon was around, she held up a finger and dialed a number. "Miss Maxwell is here to see you, sir." She hung up and said, "You can go on in. He's expecting you."

Jamie's dad always said he didn't need a stuffy office—that his workplace was the cockpit of his race car. From the looks of Butch Devalon's place, he didn't agree with her dad. His desk sat near a long window overlooking the massive garage, where he could watch the workers move back and forth among the cars. He had a video monitor about one-quarter inch thick that covered most of one wall, and the rest of the walls had pictures or trophies or pictures of trophies. Jamie didn't see one book in the whole office.

"Jamie, I'm glad to see you today," Butch Devalon said, extending a hand. "Have a seat."

Jamie settled into one of the biggest overstuffed chairs on the planet. *This must be what a baby feels like in the womb*, she thought.

"How's your dad doing today?" he said. "I'll bet he's a little sore."

"In more ways than one," Jamie said. "I don't think I've ever seen him as mad as he was last night."

Mr. Devalon nodded. "I can understand. He fought hard that whole race. Picked up a bunch of points, though."

"Dad's not into losing on the last turn."

"Well, maybe that'll teach him a valuable lesson. So, have you made a decision? Are you going to take me up on the offer?"

Jamie handed him the sheet with a check paper-clipped to the top. "I've made a deal with my mom and had meetings with my teachers. I'm all set."

"That's great," he said, looking over the application. "Everything looks just fine here. I have high hopes for you, Jamie. I've seen most of your competition, and it'll be quite a learning experience for you."

Jamie couldn't help wondering if she was walking into some kind of trap. The way the guy looked at her was beyond strange.

"Now I've got a little surprise for you," he said, standing and moving to the huge window. "You see that bright orange car down there?"

"How could I miss it?" Jamie said. "It's the only one that's not black."

He chuckled. "Well, you don't look like a black-car driver. You need something brighter to fit your personality."

"Wait, you mean . . . ?"

"Yes, that's *your* car. Here are the keys and the keys to the garage. I'm giving you full access. If you want to test it on the track out back, you can do it anytime you want, assuming we're not using it."

Jamie's mouth fell open. "I don't know what to say."

"Nothing to say. Just be ready for the toughest school of your life."

Chapter 30
Racing School

JAMIE WONDERED what she had gotten herself into as she stood outside the brick building a few miles from Lowe's Motor Speedway.

The grizzled man who stood in front of the group looked like he'd seen more than his share of NASCAR races from under a grandstand. He was short and wore a white cowboy hat that looked bigger than he was and straight-leg jeans (Jamie figured they were as old as her mom) that covered ancient boots. His voice was more of a growling drawl than an actual voice. He wore a sticker on his chest that said, "Hi, my name is Bud Watkins."

"If you were thinking this was going to be some weekend joyride camp, then you got another thing coming," Bud snarled. "And I don't care how many quarter midget races you've won or Legend races or regional this or national that or whatever you think makes you something. Just remember if you're trying to make it to the big show, you got a long way to go."

The guys in front of Jamie had their arms crossed, their sunglasses on, smiling and acting like they expected this kind of tongue-lashing.

"And you can wipe those smiles off your young faces, boys, because that's what you are. Boys."

The white teeth disappeared, and the guys shifted and shoved their hands in their back pockets like it was some kind of synchronized competition.

"You've been chosen by current drivers or people who think you *might* have what it takes," Bud continued. "I stress the word *might*. I've seen a lot of people your age who think they know everything there is to know about racing, and they get out there on the track and find out they don't know beans." He stepped forward to a dark-haired guy with a nice haircut. "I thought I told you to wipe that smile off your face."

"I'm sorry, sir. My granddaddy used to use the word *beans*, and it made me smile. Just kind of brought back some good memories." He sounded sincere.

Bud nodded and spat on the ground. "Well, it sounds like your granddaddy was a smart man." He tipped his hat back. "Now we have only one rule, and that is I make the rules. What I say goes, and if you don't like it, you go home. There's no use of tobacco products in any form here, and if I so much as find you writing the word *tobacco*, I'll ship you out. Same goes with any alcohol. If I find it in your room, I don't care whose it is, you and your roommate go home. So if you see somebody with contraband, tell me. They're gonna call you a rat or something worse, but soon you'll find out it's better to be called names than to lose the money you put into this place. If you read the fine print on that form you signed, you'll notice that you will lose all your money you put up. You also waste your sponsor's money and time and their confidence in you."

The group got really quiet the more Bud talked because everybody could tell he wasn't just talking—he meant what he said. It was interesting that he'd waited until after the parents left to talk to them.

He explained about the hotel and pointed down the road. "We have three shuttles that will be out front each morning and will leave right at 7:30. You miss the shuttle, you go home. Eat your breakfast at the hotel. They've got cereal and whatnot. Don't come to work on an empty stomach, and when I say *work*, that's what this is. It's not playtime or a social experiment—it's work, pure and simple."

A man and a woman with name tags on walked

up. "This is Connie and Glen Percell. They'll be your chaperones, living on the same floor as you. Girls will be on the third floor of the hotel, boys on the fourth. Look around and you'll see there are a lot more guys than girls, but that doesn't mean you guys will be able to get away with anything. Glen runs a tight ship.

"We don't play favorites here. You follow the rules, you drive safe, and you'll move on. Classroom work is just as important as what happens at the track. There are 43 people signed up, but we have 11 cars for the final competition. That means most of you are going home after the first two weeks. And of the 11 that make the finals, only three will actually get the coveted license you're looking for."

Jamie gulped and looked at the people around her. Most of them had come from different parts of the country, but she recognized a few from races she'd been in over the years.

"Now I want you to say your name, tell us where you're from and who your favorite driver is."

After everyone introduced themselves, they stashed their suitcases in a locked room and took a tour of the facility. The classroom and the garage were on the first floor. On the second were the simulators—a cross between a video game and an actual car—plus a media room, where they could practice their interview skills. There was a workout room and gymnasium, a pool, and a theater area on the third floor.

"Where's the popcorn?" the dark-haired guy said to Jamie.

She didn't answer and was glad because Bud overheard him and said, "You're not going to want to eat popcorn after you see what I'm about to show you. Take a seat."

Jamie found an empty row at the midpoint of the room. Everybody seemed a little antsy, not knowing what to expect.

"This is where everyone will take a look at your driving once you've been on the track," Bud said.

Everybody groaned.

"But our first video will be a little caution about what can happen out there."

Jamie had taken driver's education at school, and they showed a movie of car wrecks and what could happen when you went too fast. She'd also seen videos of race crashes. But she wasn't prepared for what came next.

"You've seen lots of bad crashes on TV, but this is video you haven't seen. Roll it."

The video played, and Jamie watched cars careening out of control, smashing into each other, some flying through the air. Chad's crash came back to her, and she had to close her eyes. When she opened them, there were close-ups of drivers being taken from vehicles—stuff they could never show on TV. The longer the movie ran, the more groans and gasps came from those around her. She knew this was supposed to scare her, but more than anything it was sickening.

When the video ended, the lights came up and Bud stood before them. "That and more can happen to you if you're not careful. You have to count the cost every time you sit in that cockpit."

"He's just trying to scare us," a girl near Jamie whispered.

"You bet I'm trying to scare you, missy. But there's a difference in scaring you with something that's made-up and something that's real. Every one of those crashes had a real person driving, and every one of those guys either died or was severely hurt. Just keep that in mind when you get out there. Now, who's hungry?" Bud rubbed his hands together and escorted them to the lunchroom.

Chapter 31
Safe-Deposit Box

TIM SETTLED INTO HIS NEW SCHOOL and life with the Maxwells. He didn't have much success making friends and even less in understanding his class work. He'd come in at the tail end of the year and was sure he'd need to repeat the same grade next year. There was just too much going over his head.

After Texas, he'd thought he'd be going to races with Dale each week, but he quickly found out the family finances didn't allow it. Dale had finished in the top 20 at Phoenix, 15th at Talladega, and just out of the top 10 at Richmond. The team felt good about the improvement, but Tim sensed something was up with the main sponsor. It was all stuff he picked up at the dinner table and from bits of conversation around the house.

He'd been living with them only a

few weeks when Dale and Mrs. Maxwell drove Jamie to Charlotte to go to some driving school. Tim could tell the minute he saw Jamie that she was athletic—which is what you have to be if you're going to make it in racing. She went for jogs with her music player and didn't come back for 45 minutes to an hour.

Tim also noticed that Jamie was about the most beautiful thing on earth, but he tried to put that out of his mind. So most of the time he tried to avoid her, but on those few occasions when she ate with the family or they went to church together, he tried not to stare.

The one person at school who seemed to take an interest in him was a girl named Cassie Strower. She said she was in Jamie's youth group and had heard about him. She invited Tim to the group, to a Bible study, and to an all-day hike. Though he was gun-shy about such groups, he almost took her up on it. He could go to church with the Maxwells and listen to the people sing and the preacher preach (and sometimes they had dramas he liked), but he couldn't bring himself to leave behind the feelings about Jeff and what had happened at the church in Florida.

Kellen was probably his best friend, even if he was only a kid. He could catch any football, baseball, or basketball pass Tim could dish out, and he loved the attention. The two would play until daylight waned, which was becoming later and later as the days got longer and the weather hotter.

One day after school Mrs. Maxwell was taking Kellen to some dentist's appointment near the city, and Tim asked if he could go along. "I'll just walk around a little bit, if that's okay."

"Sure," she said. She told him he'd need to be back in an hour.

Tim got on the family's computer and printed out a map of downtown.

When they arrived, he took off, thinking if he hurried he could get to his destination and back and not keep them waiting.

He made it to the bank named in the letter in 27 minutes, so he knew he couldn't waste time. He pulled out the key from the envelope he kept in his pocket and walked up to one of the tellers. The security guard at the front eyed Tim, but he kept going.

The teller took down his name and the box number, then asked to see some ID. Tim just had his high school ID card, so he showed her that. She disappeared into a back room and returned with a man who asked him to step to a desk.

Tim checked his watch and knew he was running out of time. "Can't I look at what's in the box?" he said.

"Well, there seems to be a discrepancy between your name and those on the approved list."

"Sir?"

"Your name isn't listed with those who can open the box."

Tim didn't want to hand the guy the letter from the law firm because it had Tyson's name on it. "The box belonged to my dad and he's dead," Tim said. He glanced at the woman who had taken his name. She was on the phone, talking in a hushed voice.

"I understand and I'm sorry," the man said. "But only those listed on the account are cleared to open the safe-deposit boxes. May I ask how you received that key?"

Tim hesitated.

"Because we only have two approved to open it—a law firm in town and a man named Tyson Slade who resides in Florida."

"Yeah, well, I'll come back another time because I have to be somewhere in a few minutes."

"Mr. Carhardt, I think it would be best if you stayed."

"No, I gotta go. Thanks anyway."

The man looked up and nodded at someone behind Tim.

When Tim turned around, a security guard was there. Tim's eyes focused on the man's shirt pocket, which bore the name *Stout*.

An appropriate name, Tim thought. This was no little teapot.

He tried to go around Mr. Stout, but the man grabbed his arm. “Come with me.” It wasn’t a request.

“But I’m gonna be late,” Tim said, and he could feel the emotion cracking his voice.

Chapter 32
Bud's Order

AFTER AN EXHAUSTING DAY (and not getting to ride in any of the cars or the simulators), Jamie ate a boxed dinner in the dining area of the hotel with the others. Everybody wanted to talk about the video they'd seen and speculate on when they'd actually get to drive.

A girl with brown hair and big brown eyes leaned over to Jamie. "My dad told me Bud used to be a really good driver, but he never made it to the cup races because of an accident."

"Did he break his personality bone?" the guy with the black hair said. "I'm Kurt Shibley," he said, reaching out a hand.

Jamie's hand was greasy with fried chicken, so she grabbed a napkin.

The girl beside her seized the opportunity and shook his hand. "Rosa Romero. Nice to meet you."

Jamie introduced herself, and the three talked about everything from their rooms to Connie and Glen to what size engines the cars had and how fast they might go.

When she'd finished her meal, Jamie excused herself and dialed her mom's cell phone.

Her mom sounded happy to hear from her, but she seemed stressed. "How did your first day go?"

Jamie told her a few details. "Mom, you don't sound like yourself. What's wrong?"

"Oh, I'm downtown with Kellen—he had a dental appointment—and Tim came along and ran off. He said he'd be back, but I can't find him anywhere."

Jamie sighed. "Well, maybe he just got interested in something and lost track of the time."

"I hope so," her mother said. "Oh, there's another call coming in. I'd better take it. Call me later?"

"Yeah, right after I get done with my homework. Talk to you then." Jamie shook her head as she hung up. When she was at home, she and her mom talked very little. Now, away and on her own, she couldn't wait to tell her mom everything about her day.

She was heading to the elevator when Connie stopped her. "Bud wants you back at the school. Pronto."

"Are they sending a shuttle?"

Connie shrugged.

Jamie waited outside for 10 minutes, then decided to walk. She needed the exercise anyway. She took off in a jog and watched for the shuttle on her way. She made it to the school in 20 minutes without seeing the shuttle pass by, but the front doors were locked. She banged on them and rang the bell, but there was no answer.

Remembering where Bud's office was, she went around the building and peered into the tinted windows. He was on the phone, so she lightly tapped on the glass, and he motioned her to the back. She waited there a few minutes, watching the sun set over the trees to the west. The crickets and frogs were out at a nearby pond, and the sound reminded her of home.

Bud opened the door. "You're late."

"I'm sorry. I waited for the shuttle, and when it didn't come, I jogged over."

"Well, you'll need to go back to the hotel and pack your stuff."

"What?"

"You heard me. Pack up your stuff. You're going home."

About the Author

CHRIS FABRY is a writer, broadcaster, and graduate of Richard Petty Driving Experience (top speed: 134.29 mph). He has written more than 50 books, including collaboration on the Left Behind: The Kids, Red Rock Mysteries, and the Wormling series.

You may have heard his voice on Focus on the Family, Moody Broadcasting, or Love Worth Finding. He has also written for *Adventures in Odyssey*, *Radio Theatre*, and *Kids Corner*.

Chris is a graduate of the W. Page Pitt School of Journalism at Marshall University in Huntington, West Virginia. He and his wife, Andrea, have nine children and live in Colorado.

RED ROCK MYSTERIES

#1 Haunted Waters

#2 Stolen Secrets

#3 Missing Pieces

#4 Wild Rescue

#5 Grave Shadows

#6 Phantom Writer

#7 Double Fault

#8 Canyon Echoes

#9 Instant Menace

#10 Escaping Darkness

#11 Windy City Danger

#12 Hollywood Holdup

#13 Hidden Riches

#14 Wind Chill

#15 Dead End

BRYCE AND ASHLEY TIMBERLINE are normal 13-year-old twins, except for one thing—they discover action-packed mystery wherever they go. Wanting to get to the bottom of any mystery, these twins find themselves on a nonstop search for truth.